POISON TOWN

ELYSSA CAMPBELL

POISON TOWN

ELYSSA CAMPBELL

James Lorimer & Company Ltd., Publishers
Toronto

Copyright © 2023 by Elyssa Campbell

James Lorimer & Company Ltd., Publishers acknowledges funding support from the Ontario Arts Council (OAC), an agency of the Government of Ontario. We acknowledge the support of the Canada Council for the Arts, which last year invested $153 million to bring the arts to Canadians throughout the country. This project has been made possible in part by the Government of Canada and with the support of Ontario Creates.

Cover design: Tyler Cleroux
Cover image: Shutterstock

Library and Archives Canada Cataloguing in Publication

Title: Poison town / Elyssa Campbell.
Names: Campbell, Elyssa, author.
Identifiers: Canadiana (print) 20230229271 | Canadiana (ebook) 2023022928X | ISBN 9781459417496 (hardcover) | ISBN 9781459417489 (softcover) | ISBN 9781459417502 (EPUB)
Classification: LCC PS8605.A5433 P65 2023 | DDC jC813/.6—dc23

Published by:	Distributed in Canada by:	Distributed in the US by:
James Lorimer & Company Ltd., Publishers	Formac Lorimer Books	Lerner Publisher Services
117 Peter Street, Suite 304	5502 Atlantic Street	241 1st Ave. N.
Toronto, ON, Canada	Halifax, NS, Canada	Minneapolis, MN, USA
M5V 0M3	B3H 1G4	55401
www.lorimer.ca	www.formac.ca	www.lernerbooks.com

Printed and bound in Canada.

To Mom, Dad, and Amy, who have always supported me.
To the King of my heart.

CHAPTER ONE

THURSDAY, MAY 12

To be fair, this was only the second time I'd been called to Principal Socks's office.

I was waiting for him to get off the phone with Mom (aka Mrs. Woods, Bio 11 and 12). It was so *hot* in here. Sweat glued my bangs to my forehead. The office was a square box with tall windows, but Principal Socks kept the blinds and windows shut, blocking out fresh air and sunlight.

Principal Socks set down the phone.

"Sorry, could you open a window?" I wiped my forehead under my bangs. My palms were sweaty too. Okay, maybe it wasn't just the air. Maybe I was a *little* anxious.

Principal Socks rubbed his eyes with his thumb and forefinger. "Addison, I hope you've been reflecting on the consequences of your little prank?" It was a question, but before I could answer he reminded me, as patronizing as ever, "You filled Priya Gill's locker with insects."

"She called me stupid," I mumbled.

"She called you stupid, so you filled her locker with —"

"Not insects. An earthworm," I interrupted. "One worm. One. I didn't *fill* her locker with them. She's totally exaggerating ..."

As I was explaining, the principal's frown deepened until his large grey eyebrows — they were as thick as his moustache — made his deep-set eyes into caves. Oops. Interrupting him had been a mistake.

"This is your second strike." Clicking a red pen, he opened a big binder of class lists and marked another X next to Addison Woods.

I wiped my sweaty palms on my jeans. My first strike had been for missing homework. One more and there would be, to quote Principal Socks, *Serious consequences, young lady*. Maybe an in-school suspension. Still, I took comfort in knowing that the name right below mine — Jamie Woods, my brother — had a full row of red Xs for absences, arguments, not turning in homework, etcetera. And all in the year since we moved to this town.

So, I was doing fine. Relatively.

"What can you do so you don't end up in my office again?" Principal Socks tried to pin me with his gaze, but I didn't look. I looked down at his yellow and green striped socks. (Hence, Principal Socks).

"Uh ..." Honestly, it had been the same quiz since kindergarten. The answer could be: a) talk it out, b) ignore Priya or c) — "We could bring it to the counsellor?"

Slowly, Socks nodded. *Ding, ding, ding! Right answer!* My shoulders sagged with relief.

"I keep my windows closed because the air in this town is ..." Socks began, unexpectedly answering my question from before.

"The air in this town is what?" I asked, curiosity pushing away my worries.

Someone knocked on the door and I twisted in my chair.

My stomach did a little flip when Mom cracked it open. "You two are almost finished?"

"Please come in, Robin." Socks waved Mom in, and waved me out.

* * *

For the next three hours — or maybe it was just ten minutes — I sat outside the principal's office, waiting for Socks and Mom to be done talking. After trying to smile at the secretary and getting a frown in return, I avoided making eye contact. She gave off Roz from *Monsters Inc.* vibes, down to the scowl, lipstick, and glasses with the little chain.

The principal's office door shut with a swish and click. Mom's shadow fell over me. I was fourteen, and just a few inches shorter than her. I was a photocopy of Mom, with my light-brown hair and bangs. We dressed alike too, comfort first. We were average height but wiry and lanky, and all muscle and bone. Dad and Jamie were taller than Mom and me, but together our family looked as alike as a pack of Germans Shepherds with blue eyes. Rough and tumble, with bruises and grass stains and broken bones. We loved science and nature and adventure — and ignoring our problems instead of talking.

"What's going on, Addie?" Mom crossed her arms and waited.

I shrugged. "Didn't you get the whole story in there?"

"There are two sides to every story." Mom inclined her head toward the hall. "Let's walk. Come on." When I didn't move, she nudged me out of my chair. I slung on my backpack and followed.

It was 3:30 p.m. and the hallways were empty. The whole school smelled faintly of compost, thanks to Mom pushing for a school-wide compost and garden program. But you usually couldn't smell it during the day because all the BO was overpowering.

My white runners squeaked on the floor, satisfying as bubble wrap. I shuffled, squeaking them as loudly as I could.

"What happened with Priya this time?" Mom asked.

Priya and her friends had been giving me trouble all year. They started little fires with laughing and teasing, but somehow *I* always ended up in detention. I was a bomb, and Priya had the detonator.

"She called me dumb."

That wasn't the whole story. I'd been asked to read a few lines of *A Midsummer Night's Dream* to the class. I'd choked, then stumbled over my words while Priya and her friends giggled.

Priya had looked at me scornfully, raised her hand, and offered, *That's all right, Mr. Turner. I can read Addie's part, too.* Then after class in the hall, while she knew I could hear, one of her friends joked, *Is she like, actually stupid or something?* and Priya had laughed.

"Are you worried she's right?" Mom asked.

"No! Of course not." The question punched me in the stomach. It was just ... school had never been my thing, even back in Vancouver. Math was hard, and English was even harder. I couldn't get along with anyone in my class, teachers included. It had taken me so long to make friends back home, and now I barely talked to most of them. Like Mom, Dad, and Jamie though, I'd always loved science, and I was on track to finish with an A-minus even with some missing homework and careless mistakes on tests.

Mom wasn't finished. "You know that Priya's wrong, Addie. You shouldn't need to prove it to her. Especially like this. What does a prank like this prove?" Her voice warmed, and I felt her smile even without looking. "You know how you can prove her wrong? Get through high school and vet tech school. You have so much potential. Don't waste it."

She'd played the vet tech card. That wasn't fair. If I wanted to be a vet, I had to stay in school. I needed good grades. For some annoying reason, tears pricked my eyes. I hid them behind a shrug. "I'm going to bike home."

"Not today," Mom said gently, but in a tone that told me there was no point arguing. "I'm done planning class for tomorrow. Let's drive home together."

* * *

The school building was bright, shiny, and new, with giant windows and two crisp, green soccer fields. The smelting company had dumped hundreds of thousands of dollars into it, just like everything else in this town, and wouldn't let anyone forget it. A granite slab below the Canadian flag in front of the school reminded every kid, teacher, and parent of our corporate sponsors.

It was a warm, wet, golden Thursday in May. Birds fluttered between the evergreen trees around the staff parking lot. The sky was hazy, but not gloomy. I sucked in a long, deep breath, and tasted faint metal — like the smell of an indoor pool. When we first moved here I thought the smell had just been smoke from the forest fires, but that wasn't it.

We moved from Vancouver to this company town in the Kootenays last fall for a job opportunity Dad couldn't pass up — despite Mom's efforts to talk him out of it. I hadn't wanted to leave Vancouver, but when we first arrived here, I'd thought we'd moved to paradise. I had freedom like never before. I could walk or bike everywhere. And the mountains. *Oh, the mountains.* They seemed to go on forever, each range peaking higher than the last. We could hike and mountain bike and rock climb in the summer. There was skiing and snowshoeing in the winter. And when the snow melted, it pooled in hidden lakes, perfect for camping and swimming.

I unlocked my bike and walked it over to our CR-V. Puddles from last night's rain were drying up all around the parking lot. They were ringed in yellow. I crouched to inspect them.

"Hey, Mom, there are those yellow rings again."

Mom glanced back. A dark look crossed her face like a cloud passing over the sun, just like the last time I'd pointed out the yellow puddles. Her lips pressed thin. I stared at her until she turned away. What was she worried about?

On the drive home, Mom said, "I know you don't want to talk, so just hear me out. Making friends is risky. Keeping them is even riskier. Friendships take work and forgiveness, because people make mistakes, and sometimes their mistakes can hurt."

Resting my chin on my hand, I frowned out the window. The road wound down the mountain, past a park, and through streets with old, single-storey houses. We'd lived here for almost a year, and I hadn't made any real friends yet. *Whatever.* Most of the kids in my grade were just drama anyway.

When we pulled into the garage, I grabbed my helmet and bike out of the trunk.

"Won't go past the park, Mom, promise! Love you!" I glided out of the driveway before Mom could add grounded to the list of consequences.

My ponytail breezed behind me. Gravel crunched under my tires. Dogs barked. Leaves swished. My beat-up, red bike was Jamie's old one and had gears and shocks and everything.

A basketball whizzed over my head. It bounced once, then rolled into the gutter. I braked with a screech and whirled, ponytail whipping over my shoulder.

"Hey, earthworm!"

Jamie. He was shooting hoops with two of his friends at a neighbour's house.

Earthworm. My gaze narrowed. News travelled fast around a town with one high school and a population of eight thousand. I was an Introvert with a capital "I." I didn't even have Instagram. Jamie had every social media app, which was terrible because he already found plenty of ways to be a jerk in real life.

Jamie had been especially nasty since we moved. Dad's fancy new job at the emissions monitoring lab kept him busy, so Jamie didn't see much of him. Plus, Jamie's asthma had started to come back, and our doctor made him quit swimming, rock climbing, cross-country, track and field, baseball, band — *everything*. I still practised and played, while Jamie sat on the bleachers doodling and sulking.

"You're not supposed to be playing basketball, *Jamison*," I snapped. "You're not supposed to be playing anything."

Jamie pulled a mocking, pouty, punchable face. He was tall like Dad, with Dad's dark brown hair and nose, too. "You're gonna tell on me to Mom?"

"*Ooh,*" came a chorus of laughter from Jamie's friends.

"Whatever." I tried to sound chill even as my face heated. "I'm not going to go running for help when your lungs explode."

Jamie jogged past me to retrieve the basketball. He made a big show of dribbling it through his legs as he passed me, then went in for a lay-up. With the ball in the air, he froze. He grabbed his throat, making choking noises. His friends laughed, and Jamie began to laugh too.

Forget Jamie. I rode off, pedalling until my feet couldn't keep up and I had to shift gears again. I took my usual route around our neighbourhood, through the grid of quiet streets, muddy back alleys, and to the sidewalk along the riverbank.

I hopped off at the top of the hill. It was a grassy strip of park, perfect for sledding in winter (if you could stop before you hit the river). In summer, when the river was low, there would usually be a dog or two that would come up to say hello, then splash through the water playing fetch.

The roar of the river couldn't quite drown out the low, steady hum of the smelter. The smelter was a factory that extracted lead, zinc, gold, and other metals from ores. It was as big as the whole town and a half. Three smokestacks towered as high as the skyscrapers back in Vancouver, pouring out grey smog. Piles of slag — the rocky waste product left over from smelting the ore — lay around it like black sand dunes.

Over a thousand people worked there, including Dad. Without the smelter, there would be no town. The town had grown around the company. What would happen if the smelter shut down? What would happen if all those office lights went dark, and the smoke-stacks stopped pouring out smog? Dad and so many others would lose their jobs. Families would leave. Schools would close. The town would really be nothing but a slag heap.

The smelter was huge, gloomy, and threatening ... but also kind of beautiful. Its thousands of orange lights flickered, and as the sun set they reflected on the river. Long shadows of poplar trees unfolded across the hill. The fiery evening sky had turned from blue to orange to violet, but there were no stars yet. Crows rose from the treeline behind the smelter. They flew over the river toward me like a vast, dark cloud, calling to each other. I smiled up at the sky, admiring them. Mom and I loved all kinds of animals, but crows were our favourite birds. They were tiny, feathered geniuses. They could solve puzzles and use tools, just like monkeys and octopuses.

I felt my smile freeze, then shrink.

The crows were struggling to fly. Not all of them, but enough to look weird, and one crow was flying lopsided. It was falling behind. *Come on,* I thought, as if I could help it just by thinking hard enough. *Come on, you can do it!*

The crow fell like a paper airplane.

I threw down my bike. I tore down the grassy hill, sliding and twisting my ankle a bit as the grass became reedy mud at the edge of the river. My heart pounded. The crow wasn't dead. It was lying in the mud, wings splayed, breathing fast and shallowly through its open beak. It looked like ... it looked like ...

It looked like when Jamie used to have asthma attacks.

The crow didn't react as I scooped it up. Ignoring the pain in my ankle, I ran back up the hill, yelling, "Jamie! Help! Help!"

I heard Jamie shout back; far away, then getting closer, "Addie? What's wrong?!"

When I crested the hill, Jamie was already there, breathing hard as if he'd sprinted the whole way. He saw me, and his eyes went wide. The terror on his face became relief ... then frustration. His eyes flashed, and he shouted, "Addie! What the —!"

Pushing the crow into his arms, I shouted over him, "You need to get it to Mom!"

"Seriously? It's just a bird," Jamie scoffed, but didn't drop it.

"It's dying! You need to get it to Mom, Jamie!" I pointed. "Take my bike." Jamie could bike faster than I could, even if I hadn't rolled my ankle. I pushed and shoved him toward my bike.

"Okay, okay!" Muttering, Jamie climbed onto his old bike and rode home as fast as he could with the crow in one arm. For the first time in his fifteen years of life, Jamie listened to me.

The crow had fallen out of the sky. But it hadn't hit anything. It was fine, then it couldn't breathe ... after it had flown directly over the smokestacks through the smog. I looked back at the smelter — the smog still rising from its stacks — and frowned.

CHAPTER TWO

I half-hobbled, half-ran back home on my twisted ankle. My bike lay on the front lawn. I pushed through the whiny, crooked iron gate into our small backyard, yelling, "Jamie? Mom?"

"Back here, Addie," came Mom's quiet voice after what felt like a thousand seconds. My heart went *thud-thud*. Mom and Jamie stood at the table with their backs to me. Mom had her hand on Jamie's shoulder, which he wasn't squirming and shrugging off — until he glanced and saw me.

"So that ambulance rush was a waste of time," Jamie said.

"Jamie," Mom said sharply. "Tone."

I hurried over and elbowed Jamie out of the way. He left, and I heard the screen door swish shut behind me.

A lifeless heap of shiny black feathers lay on the glass table. The crow's body blurred. Tears pricked my eyes. I wiped them furiously on my sleeve. It was just a bird. Why was I so emotional? I sniffed, swallowed.

"What was wrong with it?"

"There could be many reasons that it didn't make it. We don't know. Maybe it flew into a window or —"

"It *didn't*. It took off over the smelter with the others. It was fine, but then it just fell out of the sky. It couldn't breathe."

Mom's hug tensed. I untangled myself and looked up. She

was staring at nothing, lost in her thoughts, and her mouth was a tight line.

"Why did it die?"

Mom let out a long sigh. "It flew over the smokestacks. Were there other birds that were having trouble?"

I nodded. There had been.

"Flying is energy intensive," Mom explained. "Their high breathing rate makes birds sensitive to air pollution. It's possible they flew over the smokestacks at the wrong time."

"If the air can be poisonous for birds, is it dangerous for us too?" I asked slowly.

"Your dad's job is to make sure it isn't," Mom said quickly. "The birds flew directly over the smokestacks. We're not going to go breathe directly over the smokestacks."

"Right," I said. But it didn't feel right.

That evening, dinner was hard-shell tacos with ground beef and mild salsa. We called them "white people tacos." Dad had been the cook before we moved, and Jamie and I loved to help. Mom was doing her best now, but I missed Dad's cooking.

We ate dinner without Dad, as usual. I finished off one taco (with dry meat and cheese) and Mom reminded Jamie that there were no phones at the table and then confiscated it. Mom's cooking was delicious when Jamie was in trouble and not me.

Dad's truck engine rumbled, a happy sound. I watched through the large dining room window as it pulled into the driveway. Dad entered through the screen door into the kitchen, keys jangling.

Dad's new job had changed him. He'd grown a donut of pudge around his belly, which he liked to pinch. His forehead was full of wrinkles — one for every day since we moved, I figured. He was still wiry and lanky and still had his arm muscles, though. Jamie always tried to flex and compare his noodle arms to Dad's.

"Smells delicious." Dad kissed the crown of Mom's head like she always kissed mine, but Mom didn't smile like usual. Dad had to squeeze around Mom's chair at the head of the table. "How was school?"

"Busy," sighed Mom.

"Bad," I mumbled through a mouthful of salty cheese and beef. Jamie grunted.

Dad's brows lifted, but he just sat and helped himself to three tacos with loads of cheese and sour cream.

"Work?" Mom asked Dad.

"The usual," Dad said. "I saw Dr. Gill and he told me to say 'Hello,' from Priya."

Yeah, right. I stopped chewing. Priya's dad was Dad's boss and head of Dad's environmental team. Dr. Gill didn't know that Priya and I had never been on a "say hello from" basis. Certainly not after today. Our tense and robotic table conversation became tense and robotic silence. Jamie and Dad were on dish duty.

Time to face my (late) math homework. It took me a few minutes of wandering around and yelling to ask if anyone had seen my backpack to remember that I'd left it in the car.

I set up at the dining table, which was still wet from being wiped after dinner. My binder and sticky old math textbook suctioned to it. I glared hard at the assigned questions and my messy writing on lined paper. The clock in the living room ticked. Downstairs, the washing machine hummed. Jamie was arguing with Mom about his phone, and Dad was talking on the phone at his home office in the basement, which Mom said was just his man cave.

At some point I realized that I was doodling a flock of crows on the side of my paper — a bunch of little V-shapes. Mom was outside now, sipping a steaming cup of chamomile tea on the steps by the kitchen door. I could see her if I leaned to the right a little. She sat there for a long, long time.

When I finally gave up on math (it was two days late already, what could one more hurt?) and went outside, Mom wasn't on the steps anymore. The grass itched my bare feet. I followed Mom and Dad's raised voices around to the herb garden in the backyard. Mom yanked a chickweed out from her basil pot. I retreated behind the corner of the house and listened.

"It's supposed to be better now. That's the only reason I agreed to move back to this town," Mom hissed.

Guilt knotted my belly, which was still full of tacos. I shouldn't be eavesdropping, but I couldn't make myself walk away.

"Even before the 1997 upgrade, my dad said the air was fine. But it wasn't. And now ..." She sighed. "Jamie's asthma was gone."

"Not gone. You don't outgrow it."

"I know. I know. I'm just ... I can't stop worrying. What if moving here is what made it come back?" Mom's voice faded. I think Dad wrapped her in a hug.

I tiptoed through the wet grass and opened the squeaky screen door as quietly as possible. Mom's worry troubled me more than my homework or my feet, which were still itching from the grass. I scratched the bottom of my foot. I know what I saw. If Mom was worried, then I should be, too, no matter what Dad said.

What was going on?

CHAPTER THREE

FRIDAY, MAY 13

On Friday, it poured rain. The school day went by achingly slow. All I could think about was Mom and Dad and the crow. At lunch, I ate my leftover taco and went for a walk around the school campus, invincible in my yellow raincoat. I didn't feel like sitting in the hall under my locker, chatting with the people I usually sat with at lunch. I needed to be outside, listening to the rain in the trees ... and the far-off hum of the smelter. You could hear the smelter anywhere in town if you listened. I looked down at my high tops, watching puddles overflow around my feet. They were clear today.

I checked my phone. The lunch bell would be ringing soon. I had science on Friday afternoons. Unfortunately, Priya did too.

The classroom was a lab with work benches and stools instead of desks. Science was usually my favourite subject, but not today. Nothing was my favourite today. Mr. Mahaila ran through the steps of the inquiry process on the overhead projector. I wasn't listening, not until the tiny, working part of my brain alerted me to one of the worst possible things a teacher could say.

"I'll give you your groups and then you'll have the rest of class to brainstorm a topic."

A group project. Cold sweat pricked the back of my neck. I sat upright. Priya and a few other popular kids were looking around at their friends, grinning. Others were stricken like me.

The teacher began to list names.

"Addison …"

Ugh. Who would I be put with? I hoped it would be someone better at school than me. But not *too* much better.

"… and Priya."

Oh, marvellous. Quiet laughs rippled from one of Priya's friends, twisting my insides into a humiliated knot. Priya and I made eye contact. Priya's expression mirrored my own, her shock hardening into a disgusted glare a split second after mine.

Stools scraped and shuffled. People found their partners. I didn't move. A wave of honey-vanilla body spray told me Priya had come over. She pulled a stool over and sat at the bench next to me. I didn't look. Instead, I hopped down from my stool and went straight to the teacher's desk.

"You can't put us together," I said.

The teacher raised his gaze slowly from his piles and piles of papers.

"We have history," I insisted before he'd even gotten a chance to speak. "She hates my guts."

"First, I doubt that's true. Second, working with people we think we dislike helps us grow."

"But I —"

"I don't want to hear any more. I'm not going to reshuffle the groups."

"But —"

"We can have this conversation after school if you'd like?"

That shut me up. I returned to my stool. Priya was unusually quiet. She slouched, twirled a strand of wavy hair, picked at her skirt, and flip-flopped one Birkenstock. Her sugary body spray made me feel sick again.

"Hi," I said.

Priya gave me a level look, then started flipping through my science textbook, which was even older and stickier than my math one. Her nails were painted creamy white, which made the pages look extra yellow.

I slid my textbook away.

"Let's just pick a topic." Priya ran a hand over her shoulder-length, dark brown hair. Highlights streaked it, like she was Cruella de Vil lite™. "What would you like to do?"

"Die," I said. Dying sounded good right then.

"Whatever," Priya sighed.

Two of Priya's friends were glancing and giggling again. *They'd* been paired up. It wasn't fair. Priya looked over at them longingly. One girl blew her a kiss. They were having the time of their lives. This would follow me home.

"If you post this anywhere —" I threatened.

"Seriously?" Priya rolled her eyes. "I don't *care* enough about this project, or you, to put this on my story."

That was a slap to the face. Of all the mean things I expected Priya to say, she always came up with something meaner somehow. I looked away so she wouldn't see my face turning an even deeper shade of red. Priya's friends were snickering again, but there was no way they could've heard what Priya said, or seen my face. They were just like that, I guess.

"I can't work with your friends snorting behind us," I told Priya. "It's distracting."

"Same, honestly. We could go work at the public library after school," Priya said. She added quickly, "Just for an hour. Like, to get this over with."

Hmm. I looked at Priya from the corner of my eye. Had she just ... agreed? Agreed *and* invited me to hang out on a Friday? Didn't she have anything better to do on a Friday afternoon? A sleepover to host at her big house? Shopping online or at the graveyard-dead shopping mall from the eighties?

"It's Friday," I pointed out.

"Yeah, so like, nobody will see us hanging out."

My mouth hung open. Again! How did she always think of the meanest response? Especially when I could never think of a comeback. "I should've put spiders in your locker yesterday," I said. "I should've put a handful of *pregnant* spiders in your locker, and in your water bottle too."

"Hah!" A scowl twisted up Priya's face. "You think that's scary? When I visited my grandmama in India last summer, I found a spider in her basement the size of your stupid face."

Stupid face. Now *that* was predictable. A satisfied smile crept onto my stupid face. My grin only made Priya's expression stormier.

* * *

We could've walked to the library, but Priya's mom apparently didn't like Priya walking anywhere, so Mrs. Gill picked us up after school in her giant black tank. The SUV's engine rumbled. Priya sat in front, on her phone, while her mom talked on speakerphone after briefly asking Priya to be polite and introduce her new friend. Mrs. Gill's sunglasses were as big and dark as the SUV.

"This is Addie," Priya said. She didn't add, *She's not my friend.* Probably out of fear of her mom's reaction, which was fair.

Mrs. Gill continued her speakerphone conversation, steering with one hand. The other hand was a flash of long acrylic nails. She was using it to talk even faster and louder to the older woman on the phone, who I think was speaking in Punjabi while Mrs. Gill spoke in English. It was tricky trying to piece together what they were talking about, since I only understood half. Something about Priya. Her dad's job. Her older brothers. How her brothers were doing in university. Did they have girlfriends yet? I guessed Mrs. Gill was probably talking to Priya's grandmama, the one with giant spiders in her basement.

Mrs. Gill dropped us outside the public library. It was a new building with big windows on the edge of the town centre, overlooking the river. Inside, it smelled like books and fresh paint. The outside world was muted. Tense. Quiet. Like a strict librarian had told the river, smelter, and traffic, *Shush*. Every part of me itched with the urge to yell something random to break the silence.

We found a table on the first floor. Before my bum even hit the seat, Priya launched into an explanation of the assignment. "This is an inquiry project, which means the point is learning how to research. Not memorizing things. I went through and added some notes while Mr. Mahaila was giving instructions. Basically, it looks like it's up to us to choose any topic covered in our science textbook, do more research, then present. I'm thinking a trifold presentation board, not a PowerPoint."

The HVAC system hummed overhead. The library was empty on a Friday afternoon because people had better things to do. The only other person nearby was an elderly guy hunched over a novel. He kept huffing and clearing his throat. I looked up each time.

"Let's each come up with three ideas, then pick the best one." Priya stopped talking. I looked at her. She was frowning at me.

"Sounds good," I said.

Priya popped open the straw on her pink Starbucks bottle and took a long sip.

"Were you even listening to me?" Priya asked.

"Yeah," I said. We were picking a topic. I knew that.

24

"Three ideas each. At least."

"Got it." I pulled my textbook out of my backpack. It hit the table with a muffled *thud*. Priya flinched. I flipped through the earth and space section — there was an awesome picture of Saturn from the Hubble telescope — to physics and chemistry — too much math — to biology. In Grade 9, all the sciences were still grouped into one. I couldn't wait until Grade 10 when I could choose. Then I'd choose biology, hands down.

The photo on the front of the biology section was a flock of migrating crows. My stomach lurched. I flipped to the index, dragging my finger down the page until it stopped on pollution, page 137. Sometimes reading was impossible. Other times — when I was really, really interested — I couldn't stop.

POLLUTION

When harmful waste and chemicals damage the environment, it's called pollution. There are three kinds of pollution: air, water, and soil. Pollution can occur naturally (see volcanoes). Human activity also causes pollution. For example, car exhaust pollutes the air and damages the ozone layer. Garbage such as plastics pollute the oceans. One of the biggest human causes of pollution is industrial pollution: mining, smelting, foundries, and more.

A smelter. Like here. I flipped the page and jumped to the section on industrial pollution.

INDUSTRIAL POLLUTION

Industrial wastes, such as toxic slag, are sometimes dumped or spill into lakes and rivers. Industries release pollution into the air. This can harm plant and animal life, and when they mix with precipitation, this phenomenon is called acid rain.

There was a photo of a forest stripped bare and another photo of a puddle ringed in yellow. Below it, the caption read, *When sulphur dioxide emissions from this smelter in Manitoba mix with water, it forms acid rain.* My finger froze on the photo. It looked exactly like the puddles ringed in yellow I'd seen around town.

Priya's voice jolted me from the textbook. She'd been saying my name. "Addie. *Addie.*" She waved at my table spot, impatient. "Where's your brainstorm? You don't even have a piece of paper out."

"Oh, right." Duh. I pulled out my binder and snapped open the rings.

Priya's glossed lips slowly twisted into a frown. "You can't focus. Like, at all."

My eyebrows tightened in confusion. What was she talking about? I'd been nothing but focused. Maybe not on our inquiry project, but this was more important anyway.

"Yes, I can."

"Fine. You can't focus on what you're *supposed* to be doing," Priya said. "You're totally ADD."

Excuse me? She had no idea what she was talking about.

"What are you, my therapist?" I snapped. "My brother has actual ADHD. This *isn't* that. I just have more important things to do than this science project ..." I trailed off.

Did I want to tell Priya about the crow that had fallen from the sky, and about Mom and Dad's argument about pollution? Priya's dad, Dr. Gill, was Dad's boss. If anyone knew anything, he did. *Absolutely not.*

"More important things?" Priya demanded. "More important than school? Your grades? Your future?"

Woah. I'd known Priya for a year-ish, but she was like a whole different person without her friends around. She was still annoying, but this Priya cared a lot about school.

26

"You said you didn't care about this project," I challenged.

Priya opened her mouth, then clamped it shut. Squirming, she looked down at the table. Then she exploded with a splutter and I jumped. "This is so stupid!" Priya shout-whispered. She leaned across the table. "Just ask for help. Tell someone. What are you afraid of? Being labelled as learning disabled or the ADD kid or just different or something? You don't care about what people think. And you don't just *pretend* not to care about what the other girls think. You *actually* don't care. It's so annoying. It's what made me worried you were going to, like, take over the whole school ..."

"Like you'd understand being labelled different," I snapped.

Priya stared at me, open-mouthed, then laughed. "Are you serious? You try being the only Brown girl in a town of eight thousand white people. You try being the only sister with three brothers. You try living up to older brothers who got into MIT without even *trying*."

Oh. I looked at her. *Really* looked.

Priya's eye makeup glittered, and so did the highlights in her bouncy, beachy waves. She probably spent hours curling and conditioning her hair to make those curls look natural. She spent hours on her hair. Hours on Instagram. Hours studying in the public library where no one else would see her studying because they had better things to do.

Priya cared about getting good grades. She cared about what her family thought. About what the other girls thought. Priya cared a lot about what people thought about her. Priya cared a lot, and she was desperate to make it seem like she didn't. She wanted to keep up the image that she was effortlessly smart and confident and perfect. Why hadn't I noticed before?

Silence stretched until it popped like a piece of bubble gum.

"So brothers, huh?" My voice echoed in the library, too loud. "They suck."

"They *do*." Priya smiled. A little.

That little smile unlocked my trust, which I was probably going to regret.

"So yesterday a bunch of crows got messed up flying over the smokestacks. One fell right out of the sky and died. The principal's worried about the air. My mom's worried about my brother's asthma, which has come back since we moved here — that all can't be a coincidence. Also, there's acid rain leaving yellow-ringed puddles on the ground sometimes. Is it possible that the smelter's polluting the air? My dad says that shouldn't be possible since something called the ..." I screwed up my face, struggling to remember what Dad said exactly. "Since some kind of upgrade. So basically, I was wondering if you knew anything since your dad works there too?"

Priya was buffering. Little spinning wheels in big brown eyes showed that she was loading ... loading ... Then she blinked. "The 1997 upgrade?"

I nodded. That was it.

Priya rose and I followed her into the history section. She passed her water bottle to me, which I took without thinking. Teetering on her tiptoes, she slid out an old book.

I squinted at it over her shoulder. The book, called *The 1997 Upgrade*, had microscopic print. I didn't have time to read all that. I needed to know *now*. Priya saw my expression and rolled her eyes.

"I'll explain in my own words. This book is from the year they upgraded the smelter. It's the most recent one I could find. It's the only one, actually." Priya frowned up at the shelf again. "So basically, the smelter installed a fancy new flash furnace in 1997 based on Russian technology. A bunch of other companies tried to do the same thing, but kept failing and running out of money. Not us, we did it. The new furnace makes waaaay less toxic slag — and that stuff used to be dumped right into the river. The new furnace also makes waaaay less air pollution. Plus, they launched a brand-new program to test the air to make sure there's not too much pollution, and to keep kids from getting poisoned from the dust."

"That's what my dad does," I realized. "He works in the emissions monitoring lab. Environmental management."

"Yeah. So does mine." Priya glanced at me out of the corner of her eye. Her lips twitched into a smile. She added with a jibe, "Actually, he's *in charge* of it. My dad has a Ph.D. Yours has a Master's degree, probably?"

I ground my teeth to keep a straight face. A Master's degree was below a Ph.D. Why did she have to make everything a competition?

"So basically, what you're worried about is impossible." Priya closed the book. "The smelter isn't polluting the air. Well, there's still a little pollution, obviously, but it's a safe amount. Both our dads are making sure. So stop worrying!"

CHAPTER FOUR

SATURDAY, MAY 14

I couldn't stop worrying.

Maybe Priya just trusted her dad more than I did. I don't know.

On Saturday morning, I chewed on burnt slices of peanut butter toast. Burnt thanks to Jamie, who I forgot cranked the dial all the way to black. Apparently, toast had to taste like charcoal.

Dad slurped coffee from a company mug and observed the front lawn. If only I could stare hard enough to read Dad's mind. Dad had been trying to reassure Mom about the emissions and Jamie's asthma, but Mom hadn't believed him. Was he lying? *No.* Dad wouldn't lie. There was no way. Mom and Dad came down on Jamie like a ton of bricks whenever he lied, so Dad couldn't be lying ... but that wasn't the same as telling the whole truth. I had to find out what he wasn't saying.

"We should go over to Grandad's for dinner tonight," Dad declared to the lawn. He turned. "Whatya think, Addie?"

Oh, boy. Grandad was Mom's dad, but he was mostly a stranger to me and Jamie. It made sense that we hadn't seen much of Grandad when we were growing up in Vancouver, but now he was only a few-minute drive away. Grandad had lived in this town his whole life. He'd worked at the smelter. And Grandad's dad had worked at the smelter too.

I knew Grandad was a stranger was because Mom wanted it that way. We'd only visited Grandad as a family three or four times since we moved. Jamie got dropped off more often to walk Grandad's Australian Shepherd, Teddy, who was the best dog in the whole world.

"I think ..." I chose my words carefully. Dad was clearly trying to facilitate some kind of reconciliation, but it wasn't going to work. It never did. It was just going to put Mom on edge again. "What does Mom think?"

"Your mom is out jogging," Dad said. "And Jame-o is still fast asleep. I'm going to make a lasagna and take it over."

Lasagna was a carrot he was dangling in front of my nose. Everybody loved Dad's cooking more than Mom's, even Mom. But lasagna or no lasagna, Mom wouldn't be happy about a surprise visit to Grandad's. She also wouldn't appreciate being the second-to-last person to know about our dinner plans.

I was saved from having to respond when the screen door went *swish-bang*. Mom came in, breathing hard and dripping sweat like a melting candle. Frizzy brown hairs escaped her headband. She pulled out her earbuds. Dad pounced on her in the kitchen.

"What do you say we give Grandad some time with the kids this evening?" Dad asked, planting a kiss on her sweaty forehead.

Mom made an *mm-hmm* noise. "Could you drop them off?"

"I was going to make a lasagna and bring it over," Dad said slowly.

Mom stiffened. She set her water bottle down on the counter, hard. Her tone teetered on the edge of a declaration of war. "Did he invite us?"

"You know he'd never ask," Dad said pleasantly, as if he didn't notice Mom stiff with tension. It filled the kitchen and the dining room too, and goosebumps prickled up my arms. "He doesn't want to be a bother."

"I've got a lot of work to do."

"So do I ..."

They went back and forth like that for a while. Eventually, Dad wrangled Mom into agreeing to go over to Grandad's for dinner.

Tension crackled like static electricity between Mom and Dad for the rest of the day. With the house so charged, I didn't dare bring up their argument from yesterday. I did my homework — scrolled on my phone — at the table while Dad layered a lasagna. Normally, Jamie would drop everything to cook with Dad, but today he didn't help. I didn't say a word, and neither did Dad.

We drove to Grandad's house in silence. His house was almost a mansion. A big yellow mansion with three levels and a basement. The neighbourhood was full of big almost-mansions, giant magical maples, and wide winding streets with lampposts. A few of the houses listed *For Sale* signs. The neighbourhood should've been beautiful, except the roar of the smelter was loud here, and through the budding maples smokestacks towered over rows of roofs. The smelter seemed so close from this angle, like it was just the next street over, but I knew it wasn't really. It was an optical illusion.

"Dibs!" was the first word out of my mouth when we pulled into Grandad's driveway. I hopped out of the car before Dad had even turned off the engine. Jamie's footsteps crunched hot on my heels and I put on a burst of speed. Jamie shoved me aside and I tore after him, but he made it to the tire swing first.

I tore up a clump of grass and lobbed it at Jamie's head. There may have been some dirt still attached. He ignored it, so I would've thrown more, but a high-pitched bark made me whirl. A fluffy storm of grey and white loped toward me as fast as her sagging belly would let her. Teddy used to be a lightning bolt, but soon she'd be a mom. I met her halfway. Her brown and blue eyes — heterochromia, common in many herding breeds — gleamed. Her tongue lolled.

"Teddy!" I kneeled and hugged her, burying my cheek in thick fur. "You're so pregnant!"

Mom rang the doorbell. With another sharp bark, Teddy left me and went and said hello to Mom, who scratched her ears and kissed her on the head. Next, Teddy went to Jamie, who grabbed a stick and started to play tug-of-war with the Australian Shepherd from the tire swing.

The door opened with a splash of light.

"Hello! Welcome, welcome." Grandad stepped out onto the porch and waved us inside. Like Mom, Grandad was all ribs and bones. Unlike Mom, he was bald. Baldness was genetic. I liked to tease Jamie there was a fifty-fifty chance he'd go bald too.

I wrapped Grandad in a hug before kicking off my shoes and heading in. Teddy bolted through, her claws clicking on the hardwood floor. Soon I was sitting across from Jamie at the dining room table, with a slab of lasagna on my plate. Grandad cracked open a bottle of beer for himself and another for Dad.

Jamie reached for Dad's beer. "Can I have a sip?"

"No," Mom said.

Jamie slumped back. Cutlery clinked against dishes. Teddy's nose sniffed at the edge of the table and I slipped her a bit of ground beef. Dad made a disapproving noise and caught my eye. I smiled sheepishly.

"*Mm*. This is delicious," Grandad told Mom, extending an olive branch. He pointed a knife at his lasagna.

Mom made the *mm-hmm* noise, shutting down Grandad's attempt at conversation.

"Dad made it," I told Grandad.

Dim surprise lifted Grandad's wispy eyebrows. No one spoke for a while after that. I was too busy enjoying my lasagna. The squishy, cheesy, tomato-saucy flavours exploded in my mouth like a volcano. It burned the roof of my mouth like lava too. Tears swam in my eyes, so I chugged a glass of water until the ice hit me in the face.

Jamie snorted with laughter.

It took all my self-control not to throw the ice in his face.

"So swim club has started up," Dad said. "The kids are on the same team as you were, right, Robin?"

"There's only one swim club," Mom said, taking a sip of wine.

"You were a busy bee," Grandad said. "Racing and life guarding — I saw less of you in high school than when you went off to college." His efforts to make conversation with Mom reminded me of the time when Jamie and I dropped a bunch of Mentos into a flat bottle of Coca-Cola, hoping for a chemical explosion that never came.

At the words *swim club*, Jamie's fork paused. Then he pierced his lasagna with a sour expression. His longish dark brown bangs cast his glare in shadow. I spotted his expression and felt a twang of sympathy for him. Swim club was a sore topic for Jamie. Swim club and especially lifeguard training. Jamie had his Bronze Medallion and Bronze Cross and was finally old enough for the National Lifeguard course. He'd had to drop it all.

"Getting teenagers to talk is like pulling teeth," Grandad told Dad teasingly.

"Tell me about it," Dad said. "And you're right about swim practice. They're at the pool Monday, Tuesday, Wednesday, and Thursday evenings, and Sunday mornings. Addie is, I mean."

"What about your lifeguarding? You still pursuing that?" Grandad asked Jamie, whose storm cloud became even stormier.

Uh-oh. I swallowed a burning lump of lasagna and nearly choked.

"He's been taking a break for health reasons," Dad answered when Jamie didn't.

Grandad made a sympathetic noise. Neither Dad nor Grandad noticed Jamie's temper smouldering like magma.

"Asthma," Dad continued. "Hopefully it'll get under control, and you can sign up next year, right, Jamie?"

Jamie finished shovelling his last bites of lasagna. "I'm done. Thanks," he added to Dad at Mom's expectant look.

I pouted when the warm ball of fur under my sock feet rose. My feet slipped as Teddy, claws clicking, followed Jamie as he was taking his dishes into the kitchen. Then they both charged for the front door. Jamie talked to the dog in a silly, excited voice. He dribbled a slobbery soccer ball while she yipped and snapped at his heels.

"Don't run too hard!" Mom shouted as the door slammed. She sighed. Muttering to herself, she took the rest of the dishes into the kitchen.

Dad caught her arm. "You go catch up with your dad. Let me do that."

"No. You made the supper. Go on." That was that. "You, too, Addie. Spend some time with Grandad."

I didn't argue. Outside, that faint strange smell made the roof of my mouth itch. I tasted metal, or maybe bleach. The air smelled like a pool or pavement before the rain. The smelter hummed. The lead-melting stack loomed — the largest and closest to Grandad's neighbourhood. To my right, Dad and Grandad were drinking coffee on the white wooden lounge chairs on the front porch.

"Do you smell that?" I interrupted their conversation. "It smells like metal."

Grandad sniffed.

Dad shook his head. "I don't smell anything, hon." Before I could insist, he asked, "How's school? I know that's your favourite topic."

"We're doing research projects in science," I said quickly. I was sure I smelled it. In fact, I remember this smell. Sometimes Grandad's whole neighbourhood smelled like metal.

"What are you researching?" Grandad asked.

Priya and I hadn't agreed on a topic yet, but this was my chance to move the conversation back to the metal smell.

"Industrial pollution." My mouth went dry. I hated lies, even little ones. Jamie was a good liar, but not me. "Speaking of, are you sure you don't smell anything? The air always smells like this. Well not *always*, but —"

"Addie ..." Dad sighed.

"You must be talking about sulphur dioxide. I don't smell anything right now, but the stacks are right there." Grandad pointed at the stack towering over the neighbourhood. "The whole town used to smell like that when the plant was running at full capacity. I can't smell anything anymore."

Sulphur dioxide. Sulphur was one of the chemicals my textbook had mentioned. A pollutant that was toxic on its own and when mixed with water became acid rain. I remembered the photo in the textbook and the puddles around school.

"You chose this coffee blend, your sense of smell is fine," Dad told Grandad. He turned to me. "We've cleaned up the emissions. It's mostly steam coming from the stacks now, not black smoke like in the early twentieth century. The smell shouldn't be so strong anymore."

"If they've cleaned it up, why can I still smell it at all?" I asked.

"Well, we haven't succeeded in capturing more than ninety-nine percent of emissions," Dad said. "I wouldn't worry about it, Adds. Unless you're trying to sell a house." Dad pointed to a *For Sale* sign across the street. It creaked in the breeze. "The noise affects property values just as much. Plus, I don't really smell anything right now. Maybe you smell the rain, too?"

Laughter exploded from Jamie, and a yap from Teddy, as she lunged for the stick in his hand, stopping my train of thought. I resisted the urge to join, just so Teddy wouldn't remember having more fun with Jamie than with me. I could let them have their play time. She'd always love me more.

"When are her puppies due?" Dad asked.

"Overdue," Grandad said. "She'll probably have them when I'm out. She always does that. Tough girl." Teddy looked over, ears perking. Grandad said in a silly voice, "Yeah, I'm talking to you."

A warm, sunshiny feeling rose inside me. I smiled. Dad was smiling too. I sat down on the steps beside him.

"The pups are full Aussie," Grandad said.

"Which means they'll probably have their mom's eyes," I added. I loved Teddy's mismatched brown and blue eyes. I explained to Dad, "Heterochromia is common in Aussies. It's hereditary." Grandad smiled down at me, impressed, and I shrugged. "YouTube." Talking with Mom, and watching veterinary YouTube, I'd learned to use scientific terms that I'd never dare to put in an essay in a million years. Words like *heterochromia* and *hereditary*.

Grandad asked Dad, "Future veterinarian or biology teacher like her mother?"

"Vet tech," I said. I'd never wanted to be anything else.

"She's quick," Grandad said.

Dad took a sip of coffee. "She'll have to start using some of those smarts in school first."

My joy popped like a helium balloon pricked with a pin. I was right here, but they'd switched to talking about me instead of to me, like I was a child.

A company truck whooshed by on the street with muddy wheels, spraying gutter water. Jamie stumbled back from the spray, probably swearing, but I couldn't hear from the porch. Teddy went over to lap from the puddle. Gross.

A question popped into my head like a light switching on. "Why did they decide to clean it up?"

"Sorry?" Grandad asked.

"The pollution. The smell. Why'd they suddenly decide to clean it up?"

"It wasn't so sudden," Grandad said. He pointed at the stack. "There are different types of pollution."

"I know," I jumped in. "Air, land, and water."

"True, but that's not what I'm talking about. I'm talking about sulphur dioxide — that's what you smell — and lead. Sulphur dioxide was the least of our problems. For decades, the company released toxic lead into the air from its smokestacks and dumped lead-filled slag into the river. People didn't really know about that kind of thing back then, but eventually a University of British Columbia study showed that kids here in town had higher levels of lead in their blood than anywhere else in the country. That set the alarm bells off."

"Just so Grandad doesn't give you anxiety, the levels of lead and sulphur are safe now. There have been some studies, and the levels are still higher than in the rest of the country, but not nearly as high as they were."

"There's no safe level of lead for babies and youngsters. Lead can impact the development of their brains and nervous systems. Even low levels in a kid's blood or a pregnant mother's blood can increase the risk of intellectual impairment and affect a child's ability to pay attention."

"You're as bad as Addie," Dad said.

"What happened after people realized kids were being poisoned by the lead?" I asked.

"Well the community protested, and the government formed a task force to try and tackle the pollution issue and create programs to raise awareness and reduce exposure to dust. Soil remediation, community awareness programs ... yada, yada. The smelter was the real problem. As regulations were tightened by the government and smelters elsewhere in the country were forced to shut down, people began to get worried. The smelter is the beating heart of this town. Pollution or no pollution, without the smelter there's no work."

"Without the smelter, there's no town," Dad emphasized, and Grandad made a noise of agreement.

"So what did they do?"

"They tried to get a new kind of smelter up and running." There was an edge to Grandad's tone, even gruffer than his usual closed-off attitude. "That was the beginning of years and years of false starts, failed upgrades, and meddling European contractors interfering with our work — not to mention the lay-offs."

"Well, yes, but it was worth it, because in the late nineties there was a breakthrough. We finally started up the brand-new furnace," Dad said.

"The 1997 upgrade," I said.

"How'd you know about that?" Grandad asked.

"Research," I summarized with a shrug. I wasn't going to give credit to Priya.

"Grandad actually worked at the smelter at the time," Dad said, and Grandad harrumphed. "He can tell you that the 1997 upgrade was a small miracle. It turned down the tap on both lead and sulphur dioxide pollution and it kept the smelter in business." Dad looked at Grandad as if expecting him to back him up, but Grandad's frown just furrowed deeper and deeper, dragging the wrinkles down his forehead.

"A miracle. Hmm." Grandad rose stiffly. He motioned with his coffee cup to Dad's. "You'd like another?"

Dad waved to say, *No thanks.*

I waited until the door shut behind Grandad. "He doesn't seem as thrilled about the 1997 upgrade as you."

Dad shrugged. "Your Grandad's a smart man, but ... he did manual work. There are some things he might not understand." I didn't like Dad's tone. "Plus, people don't usually like change, even for the better. People will always be paranoid about things they don't fully understand. Think about nuclear power. Many people are paranoid about it, but statistically it's safer and cleaner."

No, that wasn't it at all. Frustration itched under my skin and I scratched my arm. "I heard you and Mom arguing the other day. What if Grandad's right, and the lead levels still aren't safe enough? What if Mom is right? What if the air is fine for you and me, but not for Jamie?"

Dad let out a deep sigh, like I'd just said something tiresome. We sat in a growing silence that made me feel smaller by the second. Like I was an ant in his long shadow.

"There are always risks and challenges about living so close to industry," Dad explained. "When we lived in Vancouver, there was crime and car pollution. Here, we've got minute amounts of lead and sulphur dioxide." He punched me lightly in the arm. It was more of a nudge, really. "If you really want to do your project on pollution, why don't you focus on auto pollution? I'm sure it'll be much easier to find sources. You could compare Vancouver, say, to Amsterdam — a city with more public transit."

All my thoughts were jumbled and useless. He sounded so convincing, and I felt so small in comparison. I bit my lip. Maybe Dad was right. Maybe I was just being paranoid. Dad knew what was going on better than Mom, or Grandad, or even Principal Socks. Maybe I was bored and trying to invent a problem that had already been found and solved years ago. Maybe everything was better now, and a teenager from Vancouver was the least likely to change anything. But ... I just couldn't let it go.

I buried my jumbled thoughts and headed for the tire swing. I pulled it back as far as I could, then hopped on. Grandad's house and the giant maple spun. The tire sloshed with rainwater and the rope was rough under my hands. I leaned all the way back, hair hanging and blood rushing to my head. Teddy's mismatched eyes blinked at me. Muddy water coated her muzzle.

A clear thought popped into my head. *What if the smelter still isn't safe enough, even after the upgrade?*

"Research question — is the smelter still polluting this town and is it safe?" I asked Teddy. I'd decided on a topic for our science project. Priya could take it or leave it.

CHAPTER FIVE

SUNDAY, MAY 15

At swim practice Sunday morning, my brain whirled like the water that had leaked into my goggles. Bubbles escaped my nostrils. I propelled myself through the water with freestyle. *One, two, three, breathe. Breathe. Pollution. The smelter. Jamie's asthma. Priya ... I still have to text Priya about the project. Do I even have her number? Right, she gave it to me at the library. There's the wall!*

Adrenaline shot through me, jolting me out of my daydreaming. Another stroke would have sent me slamming head-first into the wall. I flipped into a turn and pushed off instead. My hand slammed against someone's bare foot and my fingers bent awkwardly. Pain shot through my knuckles. *Sorry!* I sped up to pass them on the left.

"Addie!" Coach Jen was calling my name from the side of the pool. I stood up on the bottom. The other swimmer passed me. *Annoying.*

"Addie, watch your elbows." Jen tapped her right elbow and mimicked a proper freestyle. "Elbows *up*. Not out. Also, leave a five-second following distance."

I nodded, already forgetting what she'd said. It was freestyle. Front crawl. I'd been doing it basically since I could crawl on land, but Coach Jen always found something to nitpick. I guess that was her job.

Behind Coach, Jamie was on the bleachers, jealously sitting out. Mom usually made him come on Sundays (aka strongly encouraged and bribed him with a trip to McDonald's), probably because she didn't want him to spend his whole Sunday hibernating in the basement. He was filling his sketchbook with doodles. His drawings were weird, but he was good at it. Jamie was annoyingly good at anything he put his mind to — from sports, to art, to band, to cooking with Dad. If only he'd put his mind to, I don't know, being a decent person instead of being a colossal pain in my butt.

I pushed off the pool bottom into my freestyle.

If Jamie's asthma was flaring up because of air pollution, maybe if we figured out what was going on with the air he could go back to doing sports and be generally less annoying. Determination propelled me just a little bit faster, and I overtook the other swimmer again.

If the smelter was the source, it would only make sense to start looking there. I'd do Dad's job, but low-tech. I'd survey the area around the smelter, like scientists did on the nature shows I watched when they wanted to study a biome, or species, or the impact of pollution on either. I'd take photos of plants near the smelter and slag heaps and then compare them to photos of industrial pollution around town.

If I was wrong and Priya and Dad were right, that this was a wild goose chase — by the way, who would chase geese? Geese are evil and aggressive — which they hopefully were, then I'd find nothing. But if I was right ... I'd have scientific evidence that the smelter was still polluting.

Maybe, maybe. If, if, if. I was juggling ifs and maybes. It was time to turn some of them into real theories.

After practice, I waved and smiled goodbye to a few of the other girls who might eventually be my friends. Maybe. Whenever I tried to make friends, things always went wrong.

"Thanks for waiting around," I told Jamie when I came over. It was so quiet, I couldn't tell if he was ignoring me on purpose or just in his own head. Dripping, I fished my phone and towel out of my backpack. There was something nauseating about sending my first-ever text message to Priya Gill.

Me: Hey this is Addie. I've picked a topic.

"You know, Coach Jen's being a little harsh. I'd rate your freestyle at least a six out of ten. It's better than your other strokes." Jamie didn't look up from drawing. "Isn't your best time for the fifty-metre freestyle like thirty-two seconds?"

Dragging my towel down my face, I looked at him. My eyes narrowed. That was almost a compliment, which meant it was probably a trap.

"Thirty-two-point-seven," I admitted.

Jamie shrugged. "Case, point."

"The expression is case *and* point," I said.

Jamie looked up and frowned, vaguely frustrated. "Yeah, I know. It was a joke."

I slung my bag over my shoulder and headed to the change room, casting back, "You're not funny."

When I got out of the change room, Mom was done at the gym and waiting outside for me with Jamie. My heart skipped. Priya had texted back.

Priya: What topic?
Me: Let me show you. Are you free for like fifteen minutes? I'm going to go up to Grandad's and check it out. If you want to come.

Woah. I was proposing to meet up without thinking about it. Who was I, and what happened to the introvert Addie Woods?
Me: If not no worries

Priya: What topic??
Me: Pollution

Three dots popped up, then vanished, then appeared again.

Priya: Not this again.
Me: Just let me show you. You'll want to hear this. Plus, I have the perfect research question

Again, three dots popped up, then disappeared.

Me: We'll get an awesome grade.
Priya: I'm free after 11:00 a.m. Can my mom drop me off at your place?

I felt a spike of hope and smiled. That was unexpected, even with my pitch about grades. Time to land this airplane. When we were on the way home, and Jamie and I had Egg McMuffins in our bellies and Mom had her post-workout coffee, I asked sweetly, "Hey, Mom, can Priya come over this afternoon to work on our science project?"

"Priya," Mom said suspiciously. She looked in the rear-view mirror. "Priya Gill? I'm happy to hear you two have worked things out."

Not exactly, but I wasn't going to argue. I added, "Also, could you drive us up to Grandad's? We need to do some research there."

"Why Grandad's?"

"Our project is on industrial pollution, and Grandad lives close to the smelter, so ..." I left out the part where I planned to get as close as possible — without trespassing, of course — to one of the smokestacks and one of the slag heaps.

"Only if you can convince Jamie to come with you."

"Jamie? Why?" I asked in dismay.

"Me? Why?" Jamie asked at the same time.

"I don't want you girls hiking around back there alone," Mom said. "I'm sure Mrs. Gill will feel the same way. Is Priya in on any of this, or are you just making a unilateral decision?"

"Priya knows," I said. *Kind of.* "Jamie isn't exactly responsible. We'll probably get into more trouble if he's there."

"Take Jamie or don't go," Mom concluded.

Ugh, fine. I took a deep breath through my nostrils, fighting down my pride. "Jamie —"

"Not happening," Jamie said before I could even ask.

"Come on! It's not like you have anything better to do." I grabbed the front seat and leaned forward. "You're just going to play guitar in your room all day, or scroll through Instagram, or shoot hoops with your friends."

"You're reaaaally making me want to help you out," Jamie said sarcastically.

I slumped back in my seat with a loud, frustrated sigh.

But I didn't give up that easily.

"Please?" I asked after we parked in the carport and I was lugging my swim bag up the steps. I followed Jamie. The screen door slammed in my face.

"Please, Jamie?" I called down the stairs to the basement, where he'd disappeared.

"NO." Jamie's answer echoed from the void.

"You're the worst!" I shouted down the stairs in response.

A few minutes later, Mrs. Gill's beast of an SUV rumbled up to the curb. In the living room, I explained my idea to Priya. *Weird. Priya Gill in my house.* I scrolled through the screenshots I'd taken of what to look for. I was hoping to collect photos of sulphur dioxide damage: yellowing, black and brown spots on ferns and leaves; browning conifer needles; eroded stone; metal tarnished and stripped of paint from decades of acid rain; air that tastes like sulphur; yellow-ringed puddles, like I'd seen online and in the textbook.

I didn't know how much we'd find. Maybe we'd find nothing.

"I think this might be a crime," Priya said when I was done explaining.

"A *crime*?" I repeated.

"A crime?" Jamie's voice came from the hallway.

I turned and found him hovering there. "Jamie, how long have you been spying?"

"Thirty seconds." Jamie came in and sat in Dad's giant reclining chair. He folded his fingers and asked very seriously, in his best British villain impression, "Now what's this about crimes?"

Priya, annoyingly, laughed. I rolled my eyes and filled Jamie in. I didn't get my hopes up that he would change his mind, but I tried to be as convincing as possible. Embellishing the criminal part of the research couldn't hurt my sales pitch.

"I'm down," Jamie said when I was done. "Let's go."

"Seriously?" It took a second to register. I looked him in the eyes, trying to figure out if he was pulling my leg.

"It's not like I have anything better to do," Jamie said dryly with a shrug, but I didn't even care.

Hope and relief rose in my chest. I began to grin.

"I'm not," Priya said.

Hope went *poof*. "What?"

"I told you," Priya said. "Maybe this would've been interesting years ago, when people didn't know about air pollution and lead poisoning, but now they do and the company's cleaned up. You aren't going to find anything."

"Then, maybe you can prove that," Jamie said. "Addie can look for evidence of pollution, and you can look for a lack of evidence. That way you're taking a more unbiased approach, arguing for both sides and everything." We were listening intently, and when Jamie realized, he trailed off and looked away with a shrug. "I don't know."

"That's … genius," Priya said. "Let's do it."

I didn't know about genius, but Priya was in. I shot down the hall and popped into Mom's office. She was on a video conference. *Oops.* Before I could say a word, Mom winced and took out an earbud. She whispered, "Sorry, I can't drive you now, Addie. I'll need you to wait. This shouldn't take much longer than half an hour."

Glum, I returned to Jamie and Priya. They had been chatting about something, but stopped when I came back.

"Let's just bike there," Jamie proposed like it was that simple. "We've got four bikes. I'll use Dad's, you'll use mine, and Priya will take yours."

"Bike there?" Priya objected. "It's going to take like an hour to bike up to the smelter!"

"Google Maps says twenty minutes." Jamie showed us his phone.

"Don't forget the mountain, your old man smoker lungs, and …" I pointed at Priya.

"Me?" Priya's eyes narrowed a little. "What about me?"

"You're not exactly a cyclist," I said carefully.

Priya crossed her arms. Jamie mimicked trying to put his foot in his mouth. I picked a cushion from the couch and lobbed it full force at his head.

* * *

Five minutes later, we were wheeling the bikes out of the shed. My yellow rain jacket flapped in the wind. We'd made it halfway to the park, with Priya wobbling but keeping up and Jamie not showing signs of being out of breath, when Jamie checked his phone and said, "Uh oh."

I took out my phone too. Mom had texted on the group chat.

Mom: Where'd you all go?
Jamie: Took bikes. Will stop if it's too much.
Mom: Be safe.

A spike of annoyance shot through me. I zipped my phone in my jacket pocket and put on a burst of speed. The sidewalk wasn't wide enough for the two of us, so I had to bike on the bumpy grass. "Be safe? Really?" I shouted as I came up beside Jamie. "Why does she trust you? She really shouldn't trust you."

Jamie saluted. I fell back to Priya. She was looking ahead at Jamie with a small, day-dreamy smile. "What were you two talking about back home?"

"Hmm?" Priya noticed me, refocusing, and wobbled. I flashed out a hand instinctively, but she didn't wipe out. I repeated my question, and she shrugged. "Just our lives. I know he's in band, and art, and he used to be good when he was on the soccer team when you first moved here. Is there anything he can't do?"

I glanced over at her, probably longer than was safe to take my eyes off the grass. I remembered again how I'd come back from Mom's office and saw them chatting. *No.* They hadn't been chatting, Jamie had been listening while Priya had been smiling and talking his ear off.

"He's a pimply jerk with noodle arms," I said, eyes narrowing.

"He does *not* have noodle arms," she said defensively, smiling.

Ew. I shook myself, trying to erase the idea of Priya Gill having a crush on my jerk brother from my brain. I put on another burst of speed, passing them both.

We passed the park, winding along the river to the bridge where we had to walk our bikes across. The river thundered below and trucks roared by, slamming us with wall after wall of wind. After the bridge, it was a short ride through downtown to the mountain road, where the slope steepened.

"Addie! Wait!" Priya called ahead, her voice far back.

Ugh. I knew she wouldn't be able to keep up.

"It's not me! It's Jamie."

A flash of concern shot through me, and I braked. I did a 180 and glided back down the hill. Jamie was even farther back than Priya. I passed her and hopped off beside Jamie, who was doubled over his bike, straining his chest muscles to breathe.

The flash of concern mutated into a tiny, useless panic. "Are you okay?"

Jamie waved me off like an annoying fly, breathing fast and shallow.

"Can you breathe?"

He glared at me. *Obviously not.*

"Should I call Mom?"

"Wait," Jamie wheezed. He took his inhaler, breathing deeply. Bike wheels went *click-click-click* as Priya made it back to us. Priya and I waited, eyes wide — one minute, two, maybe five — as Jamie took his medicine. Was he going to collapse? I had no idea what to do if he did. Call 911? Or call Mom or Dad first, and then 911? Eventually, Jamie cleared his throat and said, "I'm good." He squared his shoulders and hopped back on his bike.

I planted my foot on his tire. "You're *not* good."

There was no arguing with Jamie, though, so we kept going. We took it easier, but eventually, the road levelled off and the industrial hum rose to a dull roar. The smelter was right there — huge, long, and pumping out smog. Orange lights flickered. It looked like a post-apocalyptic bunker. Heaps of slag peaked over the smelter buildings. I sniffed. The smell was getting stronger the closer we got. We continued past it, and forest replaced the smelter as we followed my map to the pit I saw on satellite view.

"It should be here." I veered off the side of the road, propping my bike against a tree when the strip of forest became too thick. Stumbling, we hiked through the forest until we came to a gravel road. Jamie's faint humming was the only sound. The silence should've been nice since we were farther away from the highway. Instead, it was unnerving.

Then, we were in front of the slag heap.

Jamie stopped humming and stared up at the black mountain. "Woah. I think we found your slag heap."

"It never looks this big from the road," Priya said.

"Shh. Listen." I raised a finger to my lips.

"I don't hear anything," Priya said.

"Exactly."

No birds in the trees behind us. No insects buzzing around. Nothing living came closer than it had to. The slag heap was in a bald patch of forest. No dandelions or even stubborn stinging nettles grew around it. Of course this stuff was toxic, but *how* toxic? Was it dangerous to *us*, or just if you were one of the poor trees by the highway, doomed to absorb polluted groundwater and dust?

I took photos of the slag heap and the lack of life around it. Then I approached. I took a plastic Ziploc bag out of my pocket, inverted it, and grabbed a small handful of the rough, gravelly slag like it was dog poop.

Priya's hand caught my arm, nearly making me drop the bag. "What are you doing?"

I jerked away with a glare. "Collecting samples."

"You can't just take that stuff," Priya insisted. "It belongs to the company."

"I'm sure no one will miss a clump of dirt." Jamie came unexpectedly to my defence and Priya zipped it.

I pocketed the plastic bag. "Let's head down to Grandad's neighbourhood."

It was a seven-minute ride to Grandad's, all downhill, across a set of train tracks. I didn't even have to pedal. Jamie led the way. He seemed to be doing better, I think. We zoomed past Grandad's house, and the smelter roar became louder. Silver maples lining the rows of fancy houses fell away, and yellowed scraggly, empty lots replaced well-kept lawns.

A soccer field and playground nested as barriers between the edge of the company property and Grandad's neighbourhood. We headed for the playground first. It was a fossil, straight out of the nineties, and definitely not up to code. Chipped red paint peeled away from a corroded merry-go-round. It flaked where I scratched it with my nail. Was this acid rain damage? I snapped photos of paint and red, bubbly metal. Later, I'd compare each sample to photos on environmentalist websites and encyclopedias in the library — or even my textbook.

Next, I walked along the edge of the forest, taking photos of trees. Once in a while I'd find a pine or a spruce with bleached needles, brown spots on ferns, or yellowed nettles, but there were healthy plants too. A seed of doubt rose in me as I stood, looking over the fence onto the company property. Whose hypothesis was right, Priya's or mine?

"Oh, there's the path." Jamie's voice just over my shoulder sounded strange, slightly out of breath. He pointed beyond the fence to an overgrown sidewalk. "Grandad says kids used to walk through here all the time in the days when they didn't know about lead poisoning. Or getting hit by a truck, I guess."

"That must have ended in a lawsuit." Priya shook her head.

"Are you okay?" I asked Jamie. He was eyeing up the fence. "Wait, what are you doing?"

"Relax." As effortlessly as a bank robber, Jamie grabbed the chain link fence and swung himself over.

I grabbed the fence and shouted, "Jamie, get back here!"

Even Priya dared to object. "You're trespassing."

"What did you say was wrong with the air again?" Jamie put a hand against the pole.

"Sulphur dioxide," I said. "Dad says the company has cleaned up, but in the old days it used to release tons of sulphur dioxide from its smokestacks. And lead dust. Now come back before you get us all in trouble."

"So it's probably too much to hope that those things don't trigger asthma?" Jamie wheezed like he was trying not to cough.

"Technically, yes," Priya said, "and technically, prolonged exposure to sulphur dioxide can make respiratory diseases develop, but it shouldn't ..."

Jamie was really having trouble. He slumped against the fence, fumbling for his inhaler.

"... be bad enough to ..." Priya's sentence trailed off.

Without thinking — and with less grace than Jamie — I clambered over the fence, jeans catching on the top and Converse getting wedged between links, and dropped down on the other side. Priya shouted something I didn't understand.

"What can I do?" I demanded.

Jamie just waved me away, taking puffs from his inhaler, but this time it wasn't working. I pressed the heels of my palms to my forehead. *Think, Addie!* 911? Was that overkill? But Mom wouldn't get here in time, and who knows if Dad would even answer his phone.

I unzipped my jacket pocket and called Grandad.

CHAPTER SIX

The hospital waiting room smelled like hand sanitizer. Ceiling lights buzzed faintly. Occasionally, someone coughed.

Grandad, Priya, and I waited in the waiting room for Jamie to come back. Waiting and waiting. Not talking about how Grandad had found us: trespassing. Me and Jamie on the wrong side of the fence, Jamie suffocating, me uselessly freaking out, and Priya frozen.

Grandad had climbed over to help Jamie climb back over to the right side of the fence. Jamie had been able to talk by that point. I think that Jamie's attack was over before Grandad even got there, but just in case, Grandad took us all to the hospital where an ER doctor saw to Jamie right away.

Finally, Grandad said, "So what were you and Jamie and ..." he looked at Priya.

"Priya," Priya introduced herself.

"... doing snooping around the smelter?"

I exchanged a glance with Priya.

"Working on our research project. Jamie got ... carried away, as usual," I said. "Do you think that air pollution might've triggered Jamie's asthma attack?"

Grandad made a noise in the back of his throat.

"I know that air pollution can trigger asthma attacks," I added.

"And that long term, it can make conditions like asthma develop, or come back if they've faded."

"I'm no doctor," Grandad said. "Remember, you biked all the way from your place, up a mountain. Exercise can trigger asthma attacks too, I'm sure."

Frustration made me ball my hands into fists on the seats beside me. Why was Grandad hiding what he really thought? I knew Mom and Grandad disagreed with Dad, but they never told me.

"Or maybe both," I said.

"Maybe." Grandad shrugged, his armour cracking.

"I believe you about the air. *And* I have evidence. Look." I showed my phone and scrolled through the photos I'd taken at the park and the forest behind the smelter. The peeled paint, eroded stone, and burnt, yellowed bushes and ferns. "I just need someone to really tell me what's going on." I looked him in the eyes. They were dark brown, not blue like Mom's or mine or Jamie's. "Please don't tell me that I won't understand."

Priya was listening intently, but at that moment the world was just me and Grandad, and the answers I knew he could give me if only he'd trust me with the truth.

Then those old brown eyes softened. "I asked almost the same question, a long time ago. I've told you about the 1997 upgrade, right?"

"Yes," I said. "When the company installed a new kind of smelter that was supposed to stop most of the pollution."

"Supposed to, indeed. I was working at the time we were trying to replace the old blast furnace with fancy new flash-smelting technology — a foreign-designed furnace installed by contractors from overseas. I believe ... the flash furnace never quite worked, so they ended up just going with a new blast furnace."

"How do you know?"

"It was my job to train people to work in the lead department. I could've written the manuals on how to operate the old blast furnace. They built the new furnace from scratch, but it didn't seem like completely new technology to me. As promised, there was a dip in emissions, thanks to recovery facilities like acid plants, monitoring systems to cut back production, and preventative measures like wind walls but ..." Grandad trailed off. "Just like the old furnace, the new furnace still polluted the air and polluted worse the older it got."

"Why didn't you say anything?" I asked.

"Because I didn't *know* I was right. I still don't. Plus, all this was above my pay grade. I convinced myself that if I was right, the cover-up was just temporary and I had to cut the scientists some slack until they got it right. Because what was the alternative? Drastically reducing production to meet the tight new government regulations? Shutting down? Millions of dollars turned into scrap metal? I convinced myself that they knew what they were doing, and I'd just make things worse. Or lose my job."

Grandad doubted himself. I knew the feeling. "Why hasn't anyone else said anything?" I asked.

"Maybe because I'm wrong, and there isn't anything to say. Or maybe for the same reasons I didn't. Plus, nobody but the engineers saw or understood the big picture. Most people didn't care to know about anything that wasn't their part of the job. Machines run everything anyway, nowadays, and it's more complicated than ever.

"You know, your mom never trusted the company either," Grandad said fondly. His gaze unfocused. He was far away, smiling at a memory of Mom. "Before the upgrade, she joined school protests with her tree-hugging friends. She tried to get me to tell her what I just told you, but I never did. In a way, it's what made her the scientist and teacher she is today."

"You didn't lie to her," I tried to help. "You didn't know if your theory was right."

Grandad's smile turned sad. He shook his head. "Not lying isn't always the same thing as telling the truth."

Priya let out a breath that was half-laugh, half-scoff. Her wavy hair hung down over her face, a frown crinkling her forehead. She was listening. Thinking. Trying to understand. Did she believe me now? Or would she still insist that Grandad was wrong?

"Dad!" came Mom's voice from the ER entrance. She rushed over to us with the force of a windstorm. Her long coat, turtleneck sweater, and heeled boots showed she'd come straight from her video meeting.

"Where's Jamie?" Mom's tone was clipped. She didn't look Grandad in the eyes.

Grandad rose stiffly to his feet and explained, but he left out the part where we'd been on the wrong side of the fence.

Soon, an ER doctor came to speak with us. Mom's shoulders and expression went from stiff to soft with relief as the doctor explained that Jamie responded well to treatment. He could go home soon, but the doctor still asked that Mom go with him to have a more detailed conversation. I made to follow Mom and the doctor, but Grandad and Priya stayed put.

"Tell Jamie goodbye from me," Grandad said.

"You can tell him yourself," I said. "The doctor said we could go see him."

Grandad just smiled, laughed a little, and waved goodbye. I stared after him, frustration prickling inside me. Why didn't he at least try to make things right with Mom? Why was he resigning himself to staying far away from her?

"My dad's here." Priya was on her phone. She didn't look at me.

"Did you tell him what we were doing?" I asked.

"Only that your brother had an asthma attack and we went to the ER with him."

I itched with the urge to ask Priya what she thought about Grandad's story. Did she believe Grandad, or did she think he was wrong, like Grandad was worried he was?

Dr. Gill and Dad arrived at the same time.

"Addie, where're Mom and Jamie?" Dad asked.

I pointed down the hall.

Priya and her dad were already leaving, but I stopped them. "Wait! Dr. Gill, can I ask you something?" I guess now I'd already asked him something.

Dr. Gill looked surprised, and maybe a bit annoyed at being delayed, but that quickly dissolved into a polite smile. He wasn't quite as tall as Dad, but with his dark navy suit he somehow seemed taller. "Of course. It's Addie, right?"

"That's right," Dad answered for me as I started to speak. He hadn't carried on to Jamie yet after all.

Now I had to think of something to ask. My mind blanked. I looked between Dad and Dr. Gill. "What is it that you do, exactly?"

"Your dad and I work with a team of twenty scientists. We've got technicians, biologists, engineers, and other chemists like your dad. Our job is to take care of the environment."

"You test the air for sulphur dioxide and lead?"

"Yes, among other things. We use the data your dad and his team collect at monitoring stations around town and in the mountains. We slow down production if there's an abnormal increase in metal or sulphur concentration due to weather conditions, and I take the data to present an air quality report to the ministry and committee meetings."

"So if there's a government inspection or you need to collect data that meets the government's newer regulations, you can just slow down production due to 'weather conditions'?" A tiny flame of confidence inside me struck to life like a match. "Or, since you're in charge of collecting and presenting data to the ministry, you can decide when, where, and how you want to test the air?"

"Addie!" Dad whispered to me, then told Dr. Gill with a sigh, "I'm sorry about my daughter's tone."

Dr. Gill waved his concern away with a smile that indicated he wasn't offended. "I sense a young investigative journalist in the making?"

"Vet tech," I said stonily.

Dr. Gill checked his watch. "Well, it's great to finally meet your youngest," he told Dad, and they exchanged goodbyes. If I'd said anything that had bothered Dr. Gill even a little, he hadn't shown it. Priya had said nothing the whole time. Dr. Gill spoke to her in Punjabi, and they left.

"I'll text you about our project later," I called to Priya as she followed her dad. Priya glanced over her shoulder but didn't say anything. Unease wormed in my belly.

"Come on. Let's go see the Jame-ster." Dad guided me down the hall. "Jamie has a talent for ending up in the hospital. There was the time he broke his ankle skateboarding back in Vancouver. And remember when he fell out of the oak in the backyard and dislocated his shoulder, but still wanted to swim at the meet on the weekend?" He was goofy and rambling, trying to distract me. Usually, it would work. Usually. I glanced back, watching as the automatic doors slid shut behind Priya and her dad.

CHAPTER SEVEN

MONDAY, MAY 16

Priya didn't respond to my texts that evening. I checked the next morning and still nothing. Anxiety flipped and fluttered in my chest. I cornered Jamie at breakfast and told him everything Grandad had told me. As Jamie listened, his expression went from sleepy, to surprised, to guarded — like he'd stopped listening and retreated into his head. But I knew he hadn't. He made ripples in his cereal with his spoon, his gaze both dark and feverishly bright at once.

"Do you think Dad knows?" Jamie asked, his voice deadly quiet.

"We need to find out!" I was thinking about going to the library and digging up everything they had on the smelter and the 1997 upgrade. I'd find evidence even Dad couldn't explain away. "Either Dad doesn't know, or he does know and he's in on it." The phrase "in on it" sounded crazy, but it was too late to stop the words tumbling out of my mouth.

Jamie breathed in sharply through his nose. "I don't know, Addie. I've got homework to do after school."

"You were so interested yesterday," I said, unable to keep surprise and disappointment from my tone.

Jamie just shrugged, infuriatingly disinterested, and finished his soggy cereal. He left early for school with Mom since he still wasn't supposed to bike to school, especially not after yesterday.

At school, I locked my bike out front and found Priya in her usual morning spot, barely thinking twice about approaching her in front of her friends. "Can we talk?" I waved to a general spot a few feet away.

"Okay?" Priya said offhandedly, but didn't move. *Right.* Behind the bored gaze she levelled at me, I spotted a flicker of worry — or maybe guilt. I saw through her act now.

"I'm going to work on the project after school if you want to join me," was all I wanted to say in front of her friends. "I have swim practice at 3:00 p.m., but I'm free afterward."

"Maybe." Priya shrugged.

What was her problem? Gaze flashing, I adjusted one strap of my backpack, and walked away before I said anything I'd regret. School went by achingly slow, and trying to work with Priya in science the last block before lunch — when she barely even spoke to me or looked at the research I showed her — was more painful and annoying than a splinter under a fingernail. After school I saw no sign of Priya, so I took my bike and went to the pool.

* * *

I left swim practice smelling like chlorine. Strands of wet, stringy hair escaped my low, messy bun, dripping down my neck. I stopped at the dollar store and bought a trifold poster board first, then headed downtown to the smelter's interpretive centre. I'd been there a few times before with Dad. There was company merchandise, books, and flyers for sale. A little video played every few minutes, explaining the history of the town and smelter back to the 1800s. The most interesting parts of the centre were the 3D models that explained the smelting process simply enough for a kid to understand, and the tours of the smelter that left from the centre.

I picked up a flyer that advertised the smelter tours: *Tours leave from the interpretive centre on select weekdays at 2:00 p.m. Minors must be accompanied by an adult.* I took it over to the desk. A tour was my best chance to get inside the smelter, even if I had no idea what I'd be looking at.

"Hello!" The elderly employee behind the desk came over and smiled. "How may I help you, miss?"

"Can you tell me more about the tours?"

"You'll have to come back with a parent or guardian if you're interested. We're all retired company employees. We start here and explain the basics of what we do up at the smelter. Then we lead you through a tour of the outside of the smelter and take a peek at the zinc plant —"

"Wait," I interrupted, "they don't take us into the lead plant? We don't get to see the furnace they replaced in 1997?"

The tour guide blinked and looked impressed, obviously not expecting a sentence like that to come from the mouth of a fourteen-year old. "Not on this tour." He laughed. "Maybe if you were a reporter or you knew someone in management, you could get a special tour. Come back with a college degree, eh?"

My plans toppled like Jenga blocks. The company was keeping us well away from the lead smelter. If they had nothing to hide, why didn't they want us there? I slid the flyer into my backpack.

"If you're interested in the lead smelting process, you can read about it on the wall there, or watch the video."

"Thanks." I backed away from the desk and walked to the section that showed the lead smelting process. I didn't have time to watch the ten-minute video, plus, I'd seen it before. This was the wrong place to look for something the company was trying to hide.

* * *

I held out hope that I'd find Priya waiting for me in the library, but that tiny flame went out when I found the library empty except for the librarian behind the front desk. Disappointment weighed down on me like my heavy backpack. *Whatever.* I gave myself a shake, trying to forget about Priya.

I asked the librarian if they had any old articles or newspapers about the 1997 upgrade or the original study about the level of lead in blood samples that incited community concern.

She made a thoughtful *tsk.* "You'd have better luck using Google Scholar or browsing the online archives." She paused, an idea creasing her face. "Actually, I might have something you'd be interested in. Wait here."

I sent Mom a quick text saying I'd be studying late at the library again, and that I'd grab something to eat downtown, to which she replied to be home before dark.

The librarian reappeared with a few old newspapers. I thanked her and took them to the nearest empty table.

UBC STUDY INDICATES TOWN CHILDREN HAVE MUCH HIGHER
BLOOD LEAD LEVELS THAN NORMAL.

It was a news report about the original blood lead study.

KID LEAD LEVELS UP AGAIN AFTER ANOTHER DRY SUMMER.

This article was from the summer of 1998, a year after the new smelter was installed. *Interesting.*

I lost track of time, moving between the printer and the table; printing, photocopying, cutting, and gluing. The table was an explosion of books, scissors, glue, and scraps of paper. I left half the poster board empty for Priya, who still wasn't responding. The sun slowly set.

"If part of your project is looking into the effects of lead exposure, one of these could be useful." The librarian spoke and I jumped. I'd been so focused I hadn't noticed her approach. She put another packet on the table. "The language is a bit difficult, but I'm sure you'd get bonus points for using peer-reviewed scientific articles."

I thanked her, even if I doubted the articles would be useful or get me bonus points. I flipped through them. The first was about lead causing miscarriage, stillbirth, or premature birth in pregnancies. The second was about the effects of lead exposure on child development and behaviour, saying it could cause inattention and hyperactivity.

Wait. I read the first two sentences over.

Exposure to lead has been widely investigated for its correlation with ADHD. This study concludes that lead exposure is likely to be causal.

It was difficult language to understand, but I got the gist. Lead. ADHD. Was it possible there was a link not just between the pollution and Jamie's asthma, but also attention problems in our family? Could Mom's family living here be the reason Jamie had inherited them?

Jamie had to see this article. I began snapping photos, then stepped back. There was just too much. He had to see everything — not just the article, but my project and the old newspapers too.

Me: Jamie, come here, you have to come see something

Jamie: Are you upstairs?

Me: The library

Jamie: You're not even home? You want me to go all the way to the library to show me something?

Me: It's important. Please!!

Jamie didn't reply for several minutes, then —

Jamie: Fine

I couldn't wait. I took my poster board and ran outside to a short concrete wall, beyond which there was a steep drop to the river. I leaned on it, looking over at the bridge, watching for either Jamie's bike or Mom's car. It was 6:30 p.m. My stomach gurgled. I'd need to grab a sub after this if I wanted the energy to finish my part of the presentation tonight. I sat on the wall and waited.

Jamie's bike whizzed over the bridge. He disappeared behind an office building, then reappeared gliding down the grassy hill.

Jamie braked and stepped off his bike. He came and sat beside me on the wall. I handed him the poster, and somewhat unexpectedly, he read it.

"What do you think?" I asked when he was finished. "And that's just the beginning. There's so much more inside the library …"

Jamie shrugged. "I don't know."

"What do you mean you don't know!?" Frustration burst my bubble of surprised silence. "The company Dad works for could be responsible for your asthma and your ADHD, *and* lying to the town!" I said. Jamie glanced down and away, his expression hard. I lowered my voice and asked, "Do you think we should go to the news with this?"

"The *news*?" Jamie passed the poster board back. He laughed, but it sounded forced. "Addie, you sound like a conspiracy theorist."

"Because there *is* a conspiracy," I insisted.

"So you say!" Jamie shouted and I flinched.

"So I say, so Mom says, so Grandad says, and so the evidence says. I have *evidence*." I slapped my poster board back into his arms and pointed at the photos, diagrams, and excerpts proving what I had to say. "Just *look*, Jamie."

Jamie did look again. He was quiet for a long moment. "I'm not going to let you get Dad in trouble." I didn't like his calm tone or the way he glanced at the river behind us.

"Give me back my project," I demanded quietly.

Jamie didn't give it back. I lunged for the poster, but Jamie blocked my arms and moved the poster out of reach.

"I said give it back!"

Jamie threw it like a Frisbee. The poster drifted, spinning and landing in the river. I couldn't move. I couldn't speak. All I could do was look at Jamie, who was frozen like I was and staring at the water, almost as if he couldn't believe what he'd just done. I felt nothing anymore, not even anger.

"I hate you," I told him. I went back to the library to gather my things and head home. All my work was gone. I'd have to start over.

CHAPTER EIGHT

TUESDAY, MAY 17

We had to turn in our project proposal by the end of the period. While the other groups finished up on their proposals, Priya and I sat together at our bench, not speaking and flipping through our textbooks. The tension between us was as thick and irritating as smog, but I couldn't say or do anything.

Mr. Mahaila came over when neither of us handed in a proposal.

"Every other group managed to come up with a research question. I haven't asked you for a first draft of your project or to begin research, just to submit a proposal. Priya, this is unlike you."

I ignored the implication that, because he'd just said that to Priya, this *was* very much like me. Priya shrank like a mouse. All her glitter and makeup and dazzle were unable to hide her fear at being called out. The teacher wasn't speaking loud enough for the whole class to hear, just the groups nearest to us. But their conversations stopped to listen because Priya never got in trouble.

"It's not my fault." Priya didn't sound like herself. She sounded tiny. "Addie had an idea, and she wouldn't do anything else. She wouldn't compromise."

"That's not fair!" I rounded on her. "I'd almost finished the whole project, but ..." I looked down, realizing how this would sound, "... it got lost."

Likely story. Someone in the class snickered softly. Mr. Mahaila frowned at me, not angry, but disappointed. He was a jury that had already decided on a guilty verdict. Of course he'd take Priya's word over mine — and Priya wasn't *completely* wrong.

Maybe Grandad was right to just keep what he thought to himself. To keep his head down and try to act and think like everyone else.

* * *

After school I found myself in the counsellor's office instead of the principal's office, thank goodness. She wanted to see if she could help me "figure out" my problems with homework and relationships, et cetera. Mom came later and agreed to have me do some screening tests like Jamie had done in elementary school. They arranged an appointment for later that week. Mom drove me to swim practice and got me Starbucks on the way home, which made everything a little more okay.

I sipped my decaf caramel macchiato. "Priya's blaming everything on me."

"I believe you," Mom said, looking both ways as she pulled out of the busy parking lot. "This is about you, not her. If the counsellor finds you have what Jamie has, wouldn't it be good to know? If not, that's fine. Either way, this will help us understand how to help you, and it will help you understand yourself." She smiled at me when we came to a stop light and she could look over. Then she said something that warmed me inside more than my scalding, sugary, caramel drink. "On another note, Teddy's puppies are coming today."

I sat straight up in my seat, nearly spewing my drink. I made myself swallow before I asked, "Can we go over and see them!?"

"Later," Mom said.

Puppies, puppies, puppies! Five goopy Australian Shepherd puppies with shut brown and blue eyes. In my mind, they were already a few weeks old and nipping, shredding, goofy bundles of fur. I was giddy. When we got home, I ran down the stairs to my room two at a time and flopped onto my double bed. It sent a gust of wind and a stack of paper flying from my bedside table. I leaned over the side of my bed and picked it up. It was some of the research from the library — the scraps that I hadn't chosen for my poster. Why hadn't I just thrown them out?

I slid off my bed and laid my research out on the carpet, separating it into categories. Sulphur dioxide or lead. Air pollution or soil and water pollution or slag. Before or after 1997. Glowing praise or critiques of the company. It looked a little like a detective's murder investigation board, minus the string.

What was I doing? I groaned, face flopping into my hands. Why was I still focused on this? Why couldn't I just let it go?

Wouldn't it be good to know? If not, that's fine. Either way, this will help us understand how to help ... I looked at my murder board again with Mom's words repeating in my head, this time about diagnosing the town instead of my brain.

Mom's voice echoed down the stairs. She was on the phone. My heart skipped. I'd been so focused I almost forgot about the puppies. Was she on the phone with Grandad? I bolted out of my room.

"All of them?" Mom sounded like she was on the brink of crying.

My legs slowed halfway up the stairs. The railing sagged as I leaned on it, but I couldn't let go. I couldn't move. If I went upstairs, I'd ask, and I'd know. Here, I didn't know. Maybe she wasn't on the phone with Grandad. Maybe ...

"No, that's all right. I'll let Addie and Jamie know, then I'll be right over." Her voice broke down to a whisper, "I'm so, so sorry, Dad." A long pause, then she said, unpractised, "I love you too."

The words shattered like a plate on the kitchen floor.

Mom hung up. She turned, her gaze flicking down to where I was frozen on the stairs.

"Teddy's puppies?" I asked. Mom shook her head. Tears, heavy and ugly and burning, rose up my throat. Mom became blurry.

Blurry Mom opened her arms. I ran up the rest of the steps and we wrapped each other tight in a hug. "I'm going to go tell Jamie," she said, rubbing my back before letting go.

All three of us climbed into the CR-V and headed to Grandad's. Jamie was deadly quiet, looking out the window. I hadn't heard him say a word since Mom told him, and it made me feel queasy.

I knew how he felt about the puppies, even if he didn't cry or show it at all, and so did Mom. Jamie and I had always showed emotion differently. I was an explosion. It was never a secret how I was feeling. Anger and tears or excitement always burst from me, uncontrollable and overwhelming. Not my brother. Jamie was an implosion. He retreated into himself, distant, angry, and cold, and it was nearly impossible to pull him out again.

At Grandad's there was a large cardboard box on the front porch. I stopped, staring until Mom's voice called me inside. She was holding the door open, waiting for me.

We found Grandad with Jamie and Teddy in the kitchen, sitting on a chair and stroking her ears while she slept at his feet. Jamie sat cross-legged and pet Teddy's head too. The air smelled like bleach and blood. I didn't ask where the puppies were — I knew what that box meant. Mom set down her purse and went to hug Grandad. Hope and surprise flickered in me. That was the first time I'd seen them hug, the first time I'd seen them act like family. I came and sat beside Teddy. She looked so peaceful. I put my hand on her soft cheek.

Abruptly, Jamie pushed to his feet and stomped away. The front door opened and shut, not quite a slam. Mom and Grandad were having a whispered conversation.

"The boy loves this dog more than life. He ... he was hoping you'd let him keep one of the puppies. Did he tell you that?"

"No, Dad. I didn't know."

"Stillborn, all of them. They were too small, and didn't look right."

I looked between them and the door, then rose to go find Jamie outside. He was sitting on the front step.

"Can I sit?" I asked.

"Go ahead," Jamie said in a tone that meant the opposite. But I sat anyway, and looked out at the road, the maples, the ivy-covered house opposite. The lead smokestack in the distance was dead and darker than the night sky. I didn't speak, and Jamie had never been so quiet.

Maybe he wasn't quiet at all, though. Maybe it was as loud inside his head as it was inside mine. Every word and worry rang like a gong.

No safe level of lead.

An image of Teddy's muzzle dripping muddy water from the company truck.

All of them ... too small ... didn't look right.

I was going to find the truth. No one would stop me or talk me out of it anymore. Not even me.

CHAPTER NINE

WEDNESDAY, MAY 18

Wednesday was even worse than Tuesday. I was working on my own now, this time on a PowerPoint that was immune to sabotage and was much less work. Still, I felt awful. Despair, I think, was a good word for it. Despair was like having the flu, but worse. In science, Priya was also working on her own. She wasn't talking to her friends.

I passed Jamie getting a lecture from one of his teachers over his lack of participation in class, then later in the day passed him in an argument with some guy over whatever. During lunch the PA called Jamison Woods down to the office, so clearly his day was as full of awfulness and despair as mine.

At swim practice, I used the awful to propel myself forward. It was working until Coach started nagging. "Addie, leave five seconds following distance between you and the next —"

That was it. "Oh, shut up! I am!" I shouted back before I could stop it, immediately wishing I could hit undo.

Coach told me to go sit on the bleachers and cool off. I was technically on a timeout, but I used the opportunity to glance at my phone. I saw a text from Mom.

Mom: Don't forget about the BBQ tonight

Oh right, the neighbourhood had a spring barbeque at the park this evening.

I didn't feel like going, but evening came anyway and soon I was carrying our blanket to set up on the beach on the river while Mom found her friends and Jamie disappeared.

Back in Vancouver, whenever we went camping, we'd stay out until it got too dark to see — even with the campfire — or the mosquitos drove us home. But that was just us. This barbeque was like nothing I'd done before. Soccer and Frisbee up on the field, spike ball on the beach, a bagpipe band warming up under the gazebo. Hamburgers and veggie burgers were being barbequed, and hot dogs and s'mores were roasted on campfires.

I finished my sixth s'more, licking the sticky marshmallow and chocolate from my burnt thumb. My stomach hurt, but it was worth it. I sat on our picnic blanket and watched the other families play. A golden retriever puppy yipped as it chased a tennis ball into the river like it didn't feel the freezing cold, and tears pricked my eyes.

Mom was chatting with a group of moms at a picnic table, one of who was herding a toddler. Jamie was nowhere to be found, probably doing something dumb. Dad was still across the river, probably finishing up work.

It was 6:30 p.m., so the smelter was a semi-abandoned, orange-lit castle on the opposite riverbank. The bank was steep and covered in forest. Above it, the turrets of the castle disappeared into the overcast sky, which was fading from bright blue-grey to the darker grey of evening.

Mom came over. "Addie, have you seen your brother?"

I shook my head. Why would I care enough to know where Jamie was? "Probably with the guys."

"Can you go find him, please? We're heading out."

Why don't you just do it, Mom? It took all my self-control not to groan and roll my eyes as I complied.

I jogged up the stairs to the soccer field and shouted, "Jamie!" But none of the dads or kids playing were Jamie or his annoying friends from the neighbourhood. I wandered along the sidewalk, watching the river, taking my sweet time. A set of steps led down to the rocks that overlooked the river, where teenagers liked to gather and drink or whatever. Broken glass crunched under my shoes.

I heard laughter, and then I saw Jamie's head of brown hair among a group of guys he hung out with and a girl I didn't recognize. I stopped on the stairs and realized Jamie and two of the guys had stripped down to their shorts, and they were standing at the edge of the rocks, over a five-metre drop to the freezing water.

Yeah, Jamie was definitely that dumb. I shouted, "Jamie!"

One of Jamie's buddies punched him in the arm and pointed at me, but Jamie ignored me. "Uh oh, little sister alert." The friend tried to reassure me, "The current is calmer here because of the rocks."

So stupid. I spluttered, "I don't care about the rocks. Jamie! The doctor said ..." What if he had another attack? What if the cold water was a shock to his lungs and he couldn't breathe, or couldn't swim? I couldn't help. I wasn't a lifeguard.

A lifeguard. I whirled and bolted up the stairs, sprinting so fast my knees wobbled. When I saw Mom, I skidded to a stop and yelled, "Mom! Jamie's going to jump into the river!" From the look on her face, Mom knew exactly what might happen and exactly what to do. She ran after me fast, and we reached the rocks together.

They'd already jumped. And something was wrong.

The group was freaking out and swearing. The girl was asking if she should call 911. One of Jamie's diving buddies was in the water, shouting at the useless friends on the rocks and a shivering, frozen, half-naked guy on the bank. He was trying to reach for Jamie, only to get whacked in the head by Jamie's flailing arms. Jamie *was* having an attack.

"Stay back!" Mom shouted at the guy in the water. She plunged in with a perfect dive and in three strong strokes she was over to Jamie. "Jamie. It's Mom. Remember your training? I can't help until you relax." She didn't approach him until he stopped flailing, then pulled him to the riverbank.

In the end, the girl did call 911, which was the right thing to do. Agonizing minutes passed, with Mom helping Jamie sit upright and take his inhaler. His pale, sweaty face and lips were deathly blue. He was getting drowsy. His eyes were closing. How long did it take an ambulance to get here? It only took ten minutes to bike to school, and it was right across from the hospital!

Three minutes and an eternity later, I saw sirens and lights. Paramedics came down the stairs to help Jamie to the ambulance.

We drove behind the ambulance, and went straight to Jamie's room as soon as we were allowed. Dad joined us, too. The doctor informed us that it was a panic attack, not an asthma attack, but Jamie was taken for treatment just in case it triggered one.

"Classic Jamie," Dad joked when Mom finished explaining what had happened. "The air is safe for Jamie, but jumping into freezing rivers might not be."

Mom gave Dad a withering glare and he coughed into his hand.

"Mom, Dad, can I have, like, thirty seconds with Addie? I need to tell her something." Jamie's voice was hoarse and quiet, but it was the longest sentence I'd heard him speak since the puppies died and it drew all our attention. Mom and Dad stepped outside.

"You know, if you're almost dying so many times for attention, it's working. Keep it up."

Jamie took a long breath, then, as if it was the hardest thing in the world, said, "I'm sorry."

Those words from Jamie felt like a static shock, as if I'd just run sock feet over carpet then touched metal. Had Mom and Dad put him up to this?

"... Why?" I asked slowly.

Jamie shrugged, then looked down and picked at his blanket. "Just — I'm sorry. I should've listened to you from the beginning, but I didn't." *True.* "And then I was an asshole and ruined your poster because I didn't want you to be right." *Also true.*

He looked up, and there was a rare, steely determination and clarity in his eyes. Sometimes it was like Jamie wasn't even there when you were talking to him, and sometimes he was more real than anyone else in the room. "If you're right and you know it, and it's important, then tell the truth. No matter what. Even if everyone wants you to be wrong. Even if they stick their fingers in their ears and go, *La-la-la-la-la.* I'll help you if I can. I'll help you talk to Dad and the whole town."

A smile rose inside me, and I let it. I almost felt like going over there and giving him a hug. Almost.

"Okay, parents, you can come back now!" I shouted instead.

CHAPTER TEN

Later that evening, Dad made hot chocolate while Jamie watched Netflix bundled in a nest of blankets on Dad's giant easy chair. He probably only watched for ten minutes before he fell asleep. I heard Mom and Dad arguing in the kitchen. Not arguing. They didn't argue, they *discussed*.

I took a long, slow sip of hot chocolate.

"It wasn't asthma this time. It was anxiety."

"This time! He has had to stop pursuing everything he loves since we got here. He had to stop living. He can't keep on like this. He needs to be free to be himself, or he's going to get himself killed." That was Mom.

"What can we do?" Dad said, exasperated.

"We can move back home, like we've been talking about," Mom said in a steely voice.

"And if it doesn't get better in a few months? Then I'd have given up this job and we'd be no better off."

Mom fell silent, then said, "What aren't you telling me?"

"Look, we've invested billions in modernization, including a new smelter. Most of the time we keep close to the air-quality benchmarks, but sometimes levels do exceed 185 parts per billion. It depends on the weather, the direction of the wind, and which part of town you're in."

"Most of the time. How often is the rest of the time? And 185 parts per billion any time isn't good enough."

"We're not where we'd like to be, and ... I don't know."

* * *

Half an hour later I found Dad downstairs in his man cave, hunched over a pile of papers. The harsh LED desk lamp was the only light on.

"Dad? What's all that?"

Dad spun in his swivel chair and dropped a packet on the table. "The truth, the whole truth, and nothing but the truth."

I went over. There were old committee reports, what looked like spreadsheets of emissions data, and the original UBC blood lead levels study.

"I mean, it's all there. All anyone on my team has to do is look at how we collected our data back then and now, why we switched the locations of monitoring stations, the times we take readings, and the scales we're using to measure emissions."

"You did listen to Mom." I looked closer.

"You were the one who convinced me to do some real digging at work."

Me? When? At my bewildered expression, Dad picked up a pile of papers to reveal a poster board that was sticking out but that I hadn't noticed. *My* poster board. Crinkled and torn in places, but still mostly readable. *How?*

"Jamie fished it out of the river and dried it out, then showed your research to me," Dad explained. "He was convincing. And you're both right. The pollution levels are better, but not as much as we like to say. Certainly not as clean as it should be with the cutting-edge smelter technology we supposedly have in the lead plant."

I couldn't believe it. "Jamie?"

"He regretted wrecking your poster," Dad said. "I told him to apologize to you when he could do it wholeheartedly, and not before."

I swallowed down a teary feeling before it grew. I had to focus. "Did you show any of this to Dr. Gill?"

"He's seen it. He's the one who writes the reports," Dad said. "However, when I asked about the inner workings of the lead smelter, he told me that that wasn't his area."

"That's not an answer."

"Yes, it is. It means he doesn't want to give an answer."

"You're going to say something now, right? Now that we know for sure that the smelter is polluting the air and it brought back Jamie's lung problems? And that it might have even caused my and Jamie's attention problems; that we might have them because Mom grew up here?"

"Say something to whom?"

"To the news! To YouTube. The government. Your bosses. A lawyer. I don't know."

"It's not so simple. We don't really know the root cause of anything Jamie has. It may have nothing to do with the smelter, Addie. Like I said, there are risks inherent to living so close to an industry, but there are risks wherever we live. Plus we really are trying to reduce emissions to hit the government's targets. Engineering is not my department, and the smelter technology is proprietary — meaning it's a secret that belongs to the company — so I can't be certain of its design no matter the external signs. I signed a contract when I got hired that prevents me from revealing details about it too."

Wait. He wasn't going to do anything? I asked, "So you're not going to help Jamie at all?"

"If his asthma doesn't get back under control," Dad sighed, "we might have to move back to Vancouver."

A couple of weeks ago, that sentence would have been terrible news because it would mean giving up my freedom. Now, it sent a wave of frustration that tied my thoughts into confused knots, but not because of anything I would lose.

"Move?" I managed to choke out. Moving was just ignoring the problem! This was our town now. Why did no one care about it?

Shaking my head, I retreated to my room and flopped on my bed. Something crinkled under my back. I pulled out the flyer from the interpretive centre. I was running around in circles collecting evidence, but like Dad said, no matter the external signs, even Grandad couldn't know what the inside of the smelter looked like.

The tour was my only chance to get inside. I just had to convince someone to come with me.

CHAPTER ELEVEN

THURSDAY, MAY 19

Mom sat with me in the counsellor's office as I ticked boxes on a checklist. Both Mom and the counsellor's silent presence put me on edge. Mom wouldn't stop bouncing her leg.

> How often do you fidget or squirm with your hands or feet when you have to sit down for a long time?
> How often do you have difficulty keeping your attention when you are doing boring or repetitive work?
> How often do you interrupt others when they are busy?

Often. Often. Very often. When I passed the test across the desk for the counsellor to add up, I was sure the results wouldn't be good.

"So," the counsellor took a deep breath, "I'm sure this doesn't come as a surprise, but these questionnaires suggest that it's likely Addison has combined-type ADHD ..."

Mom let out a breath of air through her nose.

I zoned out, reimagining the crow falling from the sky and spasming on the grass.

The crow.

Teddy's puppies.

Jamie's asthma.

Jamie's attention problems.

My attention problems.

Mom's attention problems.

Because she was just like Jamie and me. I looked at her bouncing leg. I remembered how forgetful she was, how creative she was, how impulsive she was, and how she zoned out for hours. If I had ADHD, then maybe so did she.

There was a chance that all these things were linked. That all these things were the smelter's fault. All the evidence was there, right there, and everybody in town had bits and pieces of it. We smelled the air and saw the ugly heaps of slag. So why didn't anybody try to piece together the truth?

"... ADHD is fairly common and this doesn't come with learning support, so she'll have to learn how to develop strategies rather than have the school accommodate her." The counsellor was talking about me, not to me.

"So you're saying that my learning problems aren't serious enough for the school to pay to help?"

Oh. That was it. It was always about money, wasn't it? That's how the real world worked. The counsellor had fallen silent, taken aback. Mom blinked. Maybe they hadn't even realized I was listening.

The counsellor cleared her throat, searching carefully for her words. "We do take this seriously, but the government only provides so much funding for extra learning support. An Autism diagnosis comes with funding, but ADHD does not," the counsellor explained. "There are two treatment options: therapy and medication."

That was it. Just like my diagnosis wasn't enough of a problem for the school to devote funding, the studies, rumours, health problems, and dead animals weren't enough of a problem to draw

82

the attention of the government or the community at the risk of losing money.

Just like Jamie said, I needed to make people care more about the truth than they did about money. And since Priya wasn't answering my texts and Jamie hadn't come to school today — and would probably have a fever for the rest of his life — making people care was up to me, no matter what. There was only one other person who knew enough about the smelter to help and who I trusted to care about the truth.

* * *

"He says he's out buying groceries," Mom told me. I'd asked her to text Grandad to ask if I could go over. "He says you can talk on the weekend. Why don't you just text him?"

I smiled to myself. Because I wanted her to have an excuse to text him too. Because they were talking and Mom hadn't thought twice about texting him.

"So he's at the grocery store? You can drop me off, it's on the way home." When Mom sighed, I said, "I'll walk home or get Grandad to drive me."

A few minutes later Mom pulled into the store parking lot and I hopped out. I weaved through the parked cars and pedestrians with rattling shopping carts. Inside, it smelled like fresh bread and sausages. The store was locally owned by an Italian family, and they imported everything delicious and from Italy. The Starbucks kiosk at the front ruined the effect of being locally owned. I ignored the temptation of a hot caramel macchiato.

I walked briskly through the store, peering down each aisle. Grandad's bald head was hunched over a cart in the frozen food section. He spotted me. I smiled. It must have been a suspicious smile, because he frowned. He dropped a box of frozen chicken nuggets into his cart.

"Whatya doing?" I clasped my hands behind my back.

"Buying food," Grandad said wryly. When he was grumpy, he reminded me a lot of Jamie.

"Same."

Grandad continued down the aisle and I followed, casually pretending to be interested in the frozen food.

"So, I'm just curious ... you'd know what you were looking at if you were inside the smelter, right?" I asked.

"Sure." Grandad shrugged. "If I was inside."

"So if you were inside the smelter, and if you were *really* looking this time — not trying to look the other way — would you be able to tell for sure then if the smelter's the same as the old one or if it's completely new technology like they say?" A blast of cold air washed over me as Grandad grabbed a few bags of frozen peas and dropped them in his cart.

"Uh huh," Grandad grunted.

"I'm sure you've heard the company offers public tours. The problem is, I need an adult to accompany me." I pulled the flyer from the interpretive centre out of my pocket and smacked it down on top of the peas in his cart. I bit my top and bottom lip to keep my face from showing my excitement. "I'd like you to come. You could point out and explain things that the tour guide leaves out."

Grandad stared blankly at the flyer for half an eternity, then picked it up. "Addie, you're not being subtle. I know what you're up to."

"Are you going to try to stop me?"

Grandad sighed. He handed the flyer back to me. "This tour doesn't go into the lead plant."

"I have a plan for that." It was a dumb, obvious plan, but I liked being able to say that sentence.

Grandad raised an eyebrow.

"I'm going to ask my dad's boss."

Grandad let out a sigh of relief. Clearly, he'd been worried my plan involved breaking in or something.

"Will you help?" I asked.

"Yes," Grandad said eventually. A smile burst from me, but he held up a finger. "Only if we do this safely and legally. No jumping fences. If your dad's manager or your dad says no, we don't do anything dumb. We do the regular tour."

"Deal." I pretended to spit in my palm and held out my hand.

Grandad humoured me with a handshake.

CHAPTER TWELVE

FRIDAY, MAY 20

Friday was a pro-D day, and the coming Monday was a holiday. I'd chosen one of the busiest days of the month for the tour. Two other families with kids younger than me joined us. The guide took us through the interpretive centre, and the kids were wowed by the giant 3D diagrams explaining the lead and zinc smelting process.

I kept checking my phone for a reply from Dad. He'd said he'd see what he could do about getting me and Grandad a tour of the lead plant. I didn't have Dr. Gill's number, and getting Priya to ask on my behalf had been out of the question. That left Dad.

"Still nothing?" Grandad asked, arms crossed. He'd been hemming and hawing as he watched the video that, I assumed, had several historical inaccuracies according to him. I didn't dare ask in case it became a ten-minute, one-sided conversation.

"Still nothing." I shook my head.

The tour guide finished chatting with another group and came over to Grandad and me. It took a moment, but he recognized me and smiled. "Ah, you were here the other day right? Welcome back. And who did you bring with you?"

"Just her grandad," Grandad said. He left out that, just like the guide, Grandad was a retired smelter employee. With thousands of employees, it was unlikely they'd know each other.

A little bell over the door rang. Probably another tour group. "Hello!" The guide went over. "Have you booked a tour?"

"No, I work at the smelter. Environmental management."

I knew that voice. I turned, surprised. It was Priya and her dad. I looked at Grandad, and he shrugged.

"Rajbir Gill." Dr. Gill held out his hand, and Grandad shook it.

"Good to meet you," Grandad said. "You're my son-in-law's boss. I used to work there, too. Call me Bill."

"Did you talk to my dad?" I asked Dr. Gill suspiciously.

"Yes." Dr. Gill put his hands in his pockets. He seemed cheery and casual in his navy-blue suit with no tie, like he'd just walked off the cover of a business magazine. "Priya asked for the same tour, so we might as well include you too. I'm happy to help you both succeed at your project. You're working together, right? I can't do the tour with you now, but I'm on my lunch break so I thought I'd drop by. Meet us at the main gate at 5:00 p.m. Security will let you in."

I had a million questions. Why hadn't Priya told him that we'd stopped working together? Why had Priya asked for the tour if she didn't want to know what her dad was hiding? Why was her dad offering to help at all?

"... Why?" I asked.

Dr. Gill's smile didn't waver, and he continued as if he hadn't heard my question, "I told Priya this, and now I'm telling you: due to the proprietary nature of the technology, you'll have to sign an agreement — or rather your Grandad will on your behalf — to not photograph or record anything you see."

Dr. Gill produced said agreement and handed it to Grandad. I peered over Grandad's arm. It had two sides, and tiny print. *Ah.* It was almost comforting to know that there was a catch. That way I wouldn't feel like I was stepping into a trap.

Grandad looked at me as if to say, *You still want to do this?*
I nodded.

He took a pen out of his shirt pocket and signed for us.

* * *

That evening, we drove up to the smelter. The security guard let us through the main gate after a couple of questions.

I'd never been inside. Correction, I'd never been this *far* inside.

It was like a whole city made of metal, with trucks and buildings a thousand times bigger up close than they looked from downtown. It was *giant*. It was *loud*. Thousands of machines rumbled and roared and beeped over top of one another, distant and near. Beneath it all, there was the slow, steady rumbling of the smelter itself, like a persistent earthquake. The air tasted like dust, diesel, and sulphur.

Priya, Dr. Gill, and another employee met us in the parking lot.

"We've managed to find some equipment that fits. We'll be staying well away from heavy machinery, but just in case."

It was hot in the change room, and even warmer after struggling into the protective equipment. The hard hat pinched my head. The mask cut off my peripheral vision. The coveralls weighed me down, hot and heavy like a pile of blankets. But what felt the heaviest was my phone, which I'd tucked into the large front pocket when no one was looking. I hadn't even shown Grandad. I didn't like lying, but I had to. I needed *proof*.

We climbed into a truck and drove to the lead plant. The stack loomed straight above me, like it had been waiting for me all this time. Finally, I was here. *Hello*.

The employee held open a red door for us. I thanked him on the way by. My breathing echoed in my ears, and it was hard to hear

Dr. Gill over the clanking of our boots on metal as he led us down a ramp. A tangle of pipes, tubes, and walkways hung overhead. Gravel crunched and puddles splashed under my too-big boots. We hiked up a set of stairs — *clank, clank, clank* — and into the lead smelter itself.

I'd seen the diagrams, even if I hadn't understood them, and I knew what to expect, but part of me still expected to step into a medieval forge with liquid fire pouring into vats and smoke billowing everywhere. Instead, it was just pipes and more pipes. Walkways, pipes, and tubes imprisoned a tall, vertical cylinder. The size of it was dizzying. My mask was suffocating me and my hard hat was giving me a headache.

Dr. Gill explained what we were looking at, pointing to tanks, pipes, and ducts. His vocabulary tangled in my head. *Lead sulphide concentrate. Fluxing and fuelling. Waste-heat boiler. Electrostatic precipitator.* How could anyone design something like this?

"My point is, Addie, that this is an infinitely complicated process." Dr. Gill jolted me from my trance. "Priya told me about the goal of your research project. To invent a narrative about a company town being poisoned by a powerful, indestructible industry. But that's too simple. The company and the town are made up of people trying to do their best." I looked at Priya, and she met my gaze for just a second. "You asked me why I offered you two this tour? Because this business is too complicated for a teenage activist to understand. From the policies to the smelter itself, there are too many interlocking parts, and many minds behind each. This smelter? There is so much of it I don't understand, because it's not my job. I brought you here to show you just how small we are compared to this machine. There's nothing you or I can do. The best thing to do is to not meddle with complicated things you don't completely understand."

I should've felt tiny and terrified, but I already felt so small next to the smelter that Dr. Gill couldn't possibly make me feel smaller.

"No," I said. Even inside my mask, my voice came out surer and steadier than I felt.

"No?" Dr. Gill echoed, with a breathy, masked chuckle.

"You're not telling the truth. You may not be liars outright, but you're bending the truth and it's getting vulnerable people hurt. It's poisoning the town, just a little bit, but still enough to do harm. There's no such thing as a safe level of pollution for everyone." Finally, all my doubt was gone. "My brother can't breathe. He had to quit everything, and —" I cut myself off before telling him that I blamed the smelter for our ADHD too. I didn't have proof of that. "Tell him, Priya! Tell him what happened with Jamie."

Priya looked down. She refused to meet my gaze. My heart broke a little at her rejection, but it lit an anger inside me on her behalf. Then she stood up a little straighter, face set with determination. She said, "Addie's right."

I stared at her. I couldn't believe it. She was taking my side against her dad?

"People are getting sick," she continued. "Animals, too. We have to do something. I went into this project trying to prove that Addie's theory was wrong, but she —"

"Priya," Dr. Gill sighed, patronizing and shutting Priya down. She looked away again. "I know that your heart is in the right place, but —"

"Won't you just shut up and listen to her for a second!" It came out before I could stop it. Priya and Grandad cringed, and I knew I'd gone too far. "I'm sorry," I said quietly.

A vein in Dr. Gill's forehead bulged, despite the tight, calm face he put on. He straightened and said stiffly, with a courteous smile, "Would you please remind your granddaughter that we don't tolerate that kind of language here?" It was like he was talking to a ten-year-old.

Grandad stiffened. He was as still as a statue for thirty seconds, then turned to me with a sigh. "Addie, we're guests here. Not journalists. Not detectives. Dr. Gill is doing us a courtesy by talking to us." I started to nod, face heating, but then Grandad winked. "Even back in my day, we signed a contract to treat one another with respect, to not tolerate bullying, and above all, to respect the *law*." He turned to Dr. Gill now, his tone vaguely snide, vaguely grumpy. "Dishonest reports are prohibited, aren't they?"

Oh. I realized where Grandad was going with this. I reached into my pocket, daring a glance to see if my phone was still recording. It was. I had no idea if the sound quality would be any good, since the video was mostly of the inside of my pocket, and I couldn't take off my gloves to take photos.

"I might be just a retired old labourer, but from my layman's perspective this isn't the technology we were promised. It's not what you're telling the town it is." Grandad pointed out parts of the smelter. "This is just a modern version of the traditional furnace with some new bells and whistles. This isn't a high-energy, efficient, new flash furnace with waste-free and low-emission production." He wagged a finger at Dr. Gill. "It must be tricky to catch all the emissions from this kind of furnace. How do you plan to meet emissions goals? Just by turning down the tap?"

Dr. Gill cleared his throat. "We're still working on operational improvements to meet the tighter government regulations."

Grandad snorted. "We've been 'still working on it' for decades."

"It isn't too late!" I blurted out. I guess I hadn't learned my lesson yet. "Stop lying before it gets out of control. This isn't your fault. It's so big and complicated, just like you say, and if someone from the company speaks first, the community will appreciate that. Be honest. Don't choose the cleanest places and best times and scales to monitor air quality."

"Addie's right, Dad. What if this whole cover-up thing is going to be more expensive? Why don't you continue the research for real?" Priya asked. "Maybe if the government wants you to meet their standards, they'll give you the money to fund the research again and make the new smelter really work this time."

Dr. Gill didn't reply and I couldn't see his expression behind his gear. Was he stunned? Impressed? Angry? Proud?

"That's a great idea, kiddo. You sound like a businessperson," Grandad told Priya, and she looked down at the unexpected praise. Grandad asked Dr. Gill, "What do you think, doctor? Don't you want to see if you can get the research going for real? You might not even have to disclose a thing."

Dr. Gill laughed, looking at each of us in turn. "You really think you can convince me to change company policy in such a short time?"

"People can change their minds," I said. "I changed my dad's mind, and Priya's, and I'll change yours too. I'm not scared."

"My, my, I can see that." Dr. Gill laughed again. "I appreciate your optimism." Then his laughter died. He was staring straight where my phone was peeking out. I quickly pushed it deeper into my pocket. Too late.

Even behind his mask, I could feel his anger — the full, terrifying measure of a powerful person who had been tricked crashing down on me. It wasn't the disappointment of a teacher, but the instant hatred of an enemy. It was there for a second, then gone. Because I was just a kid. I was nothing, not a real threat.

"You're recording, aren't you? Show the phone to me, please." Dr. Gill took a step forward and I took a step back, shielding my pocket with my hand. "Your Grandad signed an agreement. That video could get him in serious legal trouble, young lady." Another step forward, hand outstretched. "Let me delete the video and nothing will happen."

No, I hadn't learned my lesson. I turned and ran, my boots thudding as I tripped and stumbled across the scaffold. I had no idea where I was going, but I couldn't let him delete the video. For Jamie. For Dad. For Teddy's puppies. For Grandad. For this whole dead-end slag heap of a town.

I came to a set of stairs and my pant leg caught under my boot. My shins, my wrists, and my helmeted head slammed into metal.

"Addie!" Priya shouted miles and miles away.

My phone skidded to the edge of the walkway ... teetered ... and tipped over the edge, surely shattering on the concrete below.

I was dimly aware of loud boots stepping gingerly around me. Someone grabbed my arm and helped me to my feet. It was Dr. Gill.

"Are you okay?" There was real concern in his voice, or maybe my head had just been banged around too much.

Everything hurt, but I nodded. "Thank you," I said. "And sorry for running. That was ... weird." What had I been thinking?

Dr. Gill stopped for a moment. Then I think he laughed, or maybe his mask made a weird noise.

* * *

Security drove us back to Grandad's truck. We left through the main gate in silence, and I avoided making eye contact with the guard in the booth. When we turned off the highway onto the road to Grandad's neighbourhood, he pulled off to the side and shut off the engine. Neither of us spoke for a moment. The sun was beginning to set, sending shadows lunging this way and that. Birds sang in the maples.

I'd had the video evidence in my hands. The smelter was right there in front of me, with Grandad and Dr. Gill explaining what I was seeing. Even more painful than losing the video was the chance

I'd had — and blown — to convince Dr. Gill to tell the truth. I'd come so close. *So close.* I wiped my nose on my sleeve and turned toward the passenger window so Grandad wouldn't see my snotty tears, but it was no use.

"You did good, kiddo," Grandad said, his voice low and kind. "Sometimes, it's not enough to be right. Somehow, you need to reach hearts. Adults like Dr. Gill's and me? Our hearts are buried under a heap of worries, responsibilities, and self-interest." He sighed. My eyes and nose stopped running enough for me to look over. He rubbed his eyebrows with one hand. "Your mom once had a conversation with me like the one you had with your friend's dad back there. She was just a little older than you. I wasn't ready to listen to her. It was easier to say that she was exaggerating, that she was just being influenced by her lefty friends and getting political, like young people do. I minimized her concerns. I made her feel small and unimportant. I pushed her away. I wish I could go back in time and make it right, but I can't. Now, it might be too late."

"It's not," I said. Mom had cried with him about the puppies. That had been a glowing crack in the wall they'd built between them. There was definitely work to be done, but it wasn't too late. "That was years ago. I think she might be ready to forgive you. I think she wants to forgive you. So maybe it wouldn't hurt to tell her what you just told me?"

A proud smile warmed Grandad's face, but faded when something in the rear-view mirror caught his eye. A car rolled up and parked behind us, headlights blinking off. Dr. Gill got out. What was *he* doing here? He motioned for Grandad to roll down his window.

"You're all right?" Dr. Gill asked me.

I nodded. I'd had more than my fair share of tumbles and broken bones. This was nothing. My shins would be puffy and purple tomorrow, though.

"You know it's a good thing you lost your phone back there, because agreement or no agreement, if you posted that online you'd risk getting sued," Dr. Gill said. Grandad harrumphed. "But," Dr. Gill continued, "you're brave. You and Priya both. When she told me about your project, what you were really doing, I was conflicted. I'd never seen her so confident about something before. And the evidence she'd collected? Very thorough. You're right, about most of it. Not all, but most."

Wait, how long had Priya been on my side without me knowing? It was just like with Jamie. I didn't know what to say. "Thank you."

"I'll admit that we're not where I'd like us to be," Dr. Gill said. "But the improvements we are making are real, even if we've abandoned the development of a flash smelter for the time being."

"For the time being?" *Not forever?* "Do you think you'll try again to invent the new smelting process, one day?"

"Technically," he rubbed the bridge of his nose, "the flash smelting process has already been invented."

Wait. It had? If the technology existed, why hadn't they finished the upgrade? I glanced at Grandad. He was frowning, but beyond that, I couldn't tell whether he found this fact at all significant. I turned back to Dr. Gill, about to ask, but he held up a hand. He wasn't finished. It wouldn't be that easy.

"We weren't the only smelter in the world to try to go the flash smelting route," Dr. Gill explained. "There have been some start-ups that have successfully developed flash lead smelters — and many more start-ups that have failed. I tried to bring up the flash smelter issue before, but there was no interest. There's no guarantee that it would end differently this time, even if we design the process and equipment based on known practices."

"Wait, why?" I asked. "If it's been done before?"

"No two smelting operations are alike — the ore, the location, the products," Grandad explained.

"Plus, even if it were a guaranteed success, I sadly doubt the company would want to risk investing that much in our sector since their mining operations are much more profitable," Dr. Gill said. "Who's going to convince them that returning to a modernization project that made them lose millions in the late-nineties is a good idea — even one that would be much cleaner and more efficient?"

There was a note of genuine disappointment in his voice.

"You could," I said.

Dr. Gill stared at me, then laughed.

"I'm serious," I said. "The technology's there now, right? Maybe it's still risky and expensive, but what if doing nothing is even riskier and more expensive? I mean, if a fourteen-year old with no engineering degree figured out something's wrong, what happens if the town takes interest? If the government decides to do its own air quality or lead study?"

"It was community concern that first prompted a study back in the eighties," Grandad said.

Dr. Gill nodded slowly.

"I know," I said, "the UBC blood lead levels study." I lowered my voice. "So why don't you do something first?"

Dr. Gill made a *hmm* noise. He slapped the window and went back to his car.

CHAPTER THIRTEEN

MONDAY, MAY 23

It was a holiday, so the park was packed. The sun gleamed in the cloudless spring sky. It was warm enough that a few toddlers were trying out the water park for the first time since fall. A band warmed up in the gazebo. A soccer day camp played in the field behind me. I set up at a picnic table and handed out flyers.

"Hello! We're trying to get people interested in a health-risk assessment about pollution from the smelter," I called to a pair of middle-age women speed-walking by. They stopped. I rarely expected them to, but I'd keep asking, nonetheless. There was no other way to do this.

"You're saying we should be concerned?" one woman asked wearily. She exchanged a glance with her walking partner.

"We should all be aware about the risks of lead and sulphur dioxide in the community today. What's the risk now? What's next? There's no safe level of lead," Jamie explained with the charisma of a real estate agent. "The truth is, the last upgrade didn't actually work as planned, but now we have the technology to make it work. And we need to, to meet new government standards for air quality. To make sure the air is safe for everyone. You can go see my dad and add your names to the petition." He pointed, then waved to get Dad's attention. Dad was on the other side of the park, encouraging the community to sign a petition for another independent study on lead levels and emissions targets. Dad waved back.

Finally, the community was paying attention. They were talking, and listening. It was a start. People were impressed enough by a teenager's knowledge of blast and flash lead furnaces, the 1997 upgrade, and government benchmarks to stop and listen. Too bad my project was already late, because I'm sure I'd have gotten an A plus if I turned in all this research.

Maybe Dr. Gill was right and it was good that I hadn't made it out with the video. Shocking the town and risking legal action wasn't the right way to handle this. The smelter relied on the town, and the town relied on the smelter. Like Grandad said, we needed to reach people's hearts. We needed people to care, not just feel angry, afraid, and betrayed. And if the community and government had put pressure on the company to upgrade the smelter once before, why couldn't it happen again? Why couldn't we finish what they'd started all those years ago?

I checked the time. *Oh!* Speaking of the Gills ... I stuffed the last few flyers into my backpack.

"Where are *you* going?" Jamie asked.

"I told Priya I'd be over in the afternoon." I hopped on my bike.

Priya lived in a new modern-style house just outside of town, across the river. The smelter hummed in the background and wind bit my cheeks as I pedalled. The river reflected the sun and the trees. It was beautiful. My heart fluttered a little.

I was out of breath by the time I walked up the steps to the Gill's front porch and rang the doorbell. Maybe it was fair that Priya got drives everywhere. I pushed stringy, sweaty hair out of my face. Priya opened the door with a smile and waved me in. I slipped off my high tops. The lingering smell of cooking greeted me, warm and spicy.

We sat at the kitchen island while Priya's tiny poodle ran circles around my stool, yapping. I petted him with my toes.

Priya offered me chai in a company mug. I took it and turned it around to get a better look at the logo, then rolled my eyes. She winked as she took the seat beside me.

"So," I began, "has your dad decided if he's going to help yet?"

I'd asked the same question every time we'd met since the night at the smelter.

Priya closed her eyes and took a long sip of chai. She made a vague *hmm* noise that might have meant, *Yes,* or, *No,* or, *Mm, this chai is really good*. "He's ... worried. He told me he tried to get the company to invest in really upgrading the smelter years ago, but was told to drop it. If he decides to bring it up again, he could get in trouble." She trailed off, her expression twisted up. "I'm more worried about the town finding out that the company's been lying to them this whole time."

There was something else. I took a sip of chai, nearly burning my tongue.

"What will people think at school, now that my dad is the bad guy?" Priya asked.

I wasn't sure if I was meant to answer. "He's not the bad guy," I said. "He's doing the right thing. Plus, if he doesn't do it now, someone else will."

Priya set her mug down hard. She scowled, but her heart wasn't in it. "It's just like you to make a mess and then leave us with the clean-up."

I grinned. She'd brought up the fact that I was moving. *Ha!* She *was* going to miss me. "I'm not switching schools until next year," I promised. "Plus, it's not like we're moving back to Vancouver."

My parents *had* seriously been thinking about moving back. I wanted to believe that I'd helped convince Dad to stay. Well, not exactly *stay*. We were still moving, but just to one of the nearby towns, depending on where we found a place. Somewhere far enough away to have better air for Jamie, but close enough that dad didn't have to give up his job and I could finish the school year here. Close enough that I could keep working on getting the town's attention.

Priya arched a perfect, pencilled-in eyebrow. "You're really not going to give up, are you?"

"Nope. And next year I'll be back every weekend, or every weekend I can be."

"You *and* Jamie?" Priya asked, twirling a lock of hair.

"Seriously?" I asked, exasperated.

"Well," Priya laughed, "I'll still miss you more."

I'd miss her too, and I didn't really want to start over at a new school again. That was months away, though. We had all summer, and every summer after that. She wasn't going to get rid of us. This slag heap of a town was part of me. Deep down, I knew it always had been, and always would be.

AUTHOR'S NOTE

Addie's town was inspired by Kitimat, BC, Flin Flon, MB, and my dad's hometown of Trail, BC, a small city nestled in the mountains of the West Kootenay region. My dad still remembers how the puddles used to be ringed with yellow. When we visit, the air occasionally tastes like sulphur, and we often walk past houses where advisories declare that the soil has been found to contain hazardous levels of heavy metals. In the past, the Trail smelter released tonnes of sulphur dioxide and heavy metals into the air and dumped toxic slag into the Columbia River. More recently, however, the Trail smelter has been working alongside the community to reduce exposure to lead and has made large strides as far as emissions control.

Much of this success came after the installation of a flash lead smelter in 1997 that drastically reduced emissions and was more efficient to boot. A win-win situation. However, this breakthrough came after nearly a decade of expensive start-up failures. It worked, but what if it hadn't? What if, in Addie's town, there was a smelter upgrade like the one in Trail, BC, only this one never quite got up and running? Would the company be content to keep polluting the air and pay fines as part of the cost of doing business? Would they be open about the pollution, or would they do what was immediately convenient and try to keep it quiet?

We may like to think that environmental awareness and company practices have moved forward since the nineties everywhere, but this scenario is being replicated across Canada, like in Rouen-Noranda and Arivda, QC. Although the setting and company in *Poison Town* are fictional, the struggle to tackle pollution from smelters is real and ongoing.

SOURCES AND FURTHER READING

Blais, S. (2022, August 15). Quebec allows copper smelter in northwest to emit arsenic levels 5 times norm. *CBC/Radio-Canada*.
*Residents of Rouen-Noranda, QB, are pushing for a copper smelter to take responsibility for arsenic pollution.

Cruickshank, A. (2021, December 19). Lead pollution hung over Trail, B.C., for nearly a century. 30 years later, the city's still cleaning up. *Canada's National Observer*.
* A history of industrial pollution has ongoing effects in Trail, BC, but the Trail smelter and community are making successful efforts to clean up the pollution.

Hertzman, C., Ames, N., Ward, H., Kelly, S., & Yates, C. (1990). (rep.). Trail Lead Study Report.

Kurjata, A., & Batchelor, R. (2016, August 24). Bad air from Rio Tinto aluminum smelter forcing her to move, Kitimat resident says. *CBC/ Radio-Canada*.
*An aluminum smelter in Kitimat, BC, sulphur dioxide, and asthma

Naylor, J. (2017, February 20). When the smoke stopped: The shutdown of the Flin Flon smelter. *Flin Flon Reminder*.
* A copper smelter in Manitoba shut down following tighter government air quality guidelines.

The Trail Area Health & Environment Committee (THEC)

Yakabuski, K. (2023, May 10). Rio Tinto's century-old Quebec aluminum smelter is living on borrowed time. *The Globe and Mail.*